THE FOURTH KEY

KATHLEEN JUDD

Ordering Information:

Prime Seven Media
518 Landmann St.
Tomah City, WI 54660

Printed in the United States of America

TABLE OF CONTENTS

PROLOGUE

Tariffa Bay on the straights of Gibraltar

The car containing two Guardia Civil pulled into the pines for a rest. The trees gave some respite from the incredible Spanish heat. Walking through the narrow strip was not easy, only the tree roots prevented the sand from blowing further inland and moving the beach completely. The winds west of Tariffa were strong even in late August, during the winter standing on the seashore meant being sandblasted.

The chance to have a quiet smoke and drink where the Captain couldn't hassle you was worth the unpleasant duty of checking the beaches. At least it was daylight, waiting there at night could be boring, as the sound of an illegal landing from the straights was covered by the noise of the pounding surf and the howling wind. Learning you missed a shipment was not something you wanted to experience when faced with Captain Gonzales in a temper.

Normally anything landed was taken away the same night unless the Guardia had a patrol there, in which case they hid it among the tree roots and covered the shipment with sand ready to retrieve when the coast was clear.

Gradually they made a half-hearted search of the woods, ending at the edge of the beach. Nothing. Oh well, back to the car and move further on.

"Is that a boat?"
"Where?
"On the edge of the sea."
"Probably rubbish but we'd better check it."

The sand was soft and tiring to walk on, but as they grew nearer they were both silent. A body lay on the edge of the sand. It was not decomposed or bloated so it had not been in the sea for very long, but it was a youngish man who was very definitely dead.

"One of us needs to fetch the wagon."
"We can't leave it here alone. I'll toss you for it."
"You always win. I think you have a loaded coin."
"You go then." he laughed. *"But leave me the bottle and your cigarettes, I've finished mine."*

Back at headquarters they stared down at the body where it lay on the table. The doctor had not spent much time on the cadaver as yet. His clothes had been removed but there was nothing to identify him. Even the labels had been removed from the clothing so they had no idea where he had come from.

"Well it appears he was dead or at least unconscious when he went into the sea. Probably from a passing boat. I would suggest he fell and hit his head before being washed overboard, except for the lack of identification and the marks around his neck. I'll perhaps know a little more when I have examined him further." The doctor looked sadly down at the deceased.

"A smuggler who fell overboard?" Captain Gonzales suggested.

"Possibly, but he is very white. Not a local or North African. Could be a tourist, I suppose."

"Why would a holidaymaker have nothing which could identify him?"

"Exactly. I need to take a good look at the indent in his skull. It could be that his identity was removed after the skull was hit but before someone tossed him overboard. But why leave his chain around his neck. If it was a neck chain he was wearing."

"That sounds bad. We'll need to check if anyone is missing. Perhaps a boat that called in at Gibraltar, although that might take some diplomacy."

Although enquiries were made, nobody admitted to having lost anyone. The body was photographed and buried before the heat caused putrefaction.

CHAPTER ONE

Bournemouth - August 1966

he house was one of many similar in a leafy road of the seaside town. Most of the larger ones had a sign advertising a hotel or boarding house such as Sea View, or Sandy Lodge, but this one was slightly smaller and had no sign. Most of the front gardens were now parking areas for the ever increasing amount of holiday makers who arrived by car rather than by special holiday trains or coaches, as had been usual in the past. There was a parking area at the front of this house, but it was only for a couple of cars and was fairly hidden by the somewhat overgrown shrubbery.

Most of the houses had a porch to protect from the stiff breeze off the sea and this house was no different. What was different could be seen when you came through the front door into the normally large hall with its obligatory side table flanked by upright chairs. To the right hand side was the impressive oak door to the front lounge and facing it a door to a downstairs cloakroom for anyone caught short while waiting. Where the hall continued to the staircase there was a sturdy wooden partition with a very obviously locked door. Anyone entering this house was not welcome any further.

Usually anyone who visited had an appointment. There was a brass bell push outside with the request 'Please ring for attention' as the front door was often shut for security. Beside the bell was a small brass plaque announcing 'Williams, Mathers and Phelps, Private Investigators'.

The agency had only been operating for six months and spent most of their time finding lost or stolen cats and dogs, or the whereabouts of estranged offspring who were old enough to leave home and did so after an unfortunate argument. Most of the parents regretted what had been said and only wished to know their children were safe and knew of their change of heart.

The most unusual feature of this agency was that all three of those listed on the plaque were still in their early twenties.

When the telephone rang, Janine Mathers, sitting at the large desk in the front parlour which served as their office, answered with confidence.

"Williams, Mathers and Phelps. How can I help you?"

Normally the person on the other end of the phone was reticent, or at least tongue tied, never having employed such an agency before. This time the voice was that of a confident male.

"Am I speaking to Janine Mathers?" He enquired.

"You are, sir. How can I help?"

"I wish to employ your agency but I need to speak to all three of you at the same time. When will you be available? The matter is extremely urgent."

"Mr Williams usually only works at the weekend, sir."

"Is he not available before that? Does he not live in the building?"

Janine was a little worried at the stranger knowing such information.

"If it is very urgent, we will all three be here this evening after working hours. Say seven thirty. May I have your name, sir?"

"Good. I will be with you then." The phone clicked and Janine was left holding a buzzing receiver.

Neil Phelps was the first to arrive home having had a frustrating day at the town hall in Brighton trying to find if a missing son was on the voting register. They had been very reticent to give him any information, believing him to be too young to be who he said he was. It had taken a deal of persuasion for them to phone Bournemouth Police and speak to Inspector Dutton who could vouch for him.

"Have we heard from Bournemouth Police about being given some kind of registered identity card?" Neil threw himself into the elderly armchair in the private living room.

"I gather you had problems again?" Janine looked sympathetic.

"I had to get Brighton town hall to phone Dutton to vouch for me. It's ridiculous. If the Police are happy to recommend us for cases they don't cover, then we should have some kind of pass to prove who we are."

"I have contacted them but I will phone again. It depends on the Chief Constable apparently and he is new."

"Tell them it will save them being contacted on a daily basis to verify who I am. What time is Roger due home?"

"Soon, I hope. I did ask him to pick up some groceries on his way home. With only me in the office it does restrict me where shopping is concerned."

"Whose turn is it to cook?"

Janine laughed. "Roger's. I think a cooked meal may be included in with the shopping. I just hope he isn't too long."

"Why, do we need to discuss something?"

"Yes. Well. Actually, someone phoned. He is coming at seven thirty. He insisted we all three needed to be here."

Neil frowned. "Who is he?"

"That's the problem, I don't know. I did ask his name but he put the phone down without answering me. He knew who we were, Neil. He called me Janine and knew Roger lived here."

Neil frowned. "We need to be careful."

"I know. I'm worried Neil."

"Worried or frightened, Janie?"

Janine chewed her lip. "I suppose I'm still rather nervous. At least all three of us will be there. It's not like during the day when there is usually only me."

"I've told you. When someone makes an appointment I will arrange to be here."

"That rather defeats the plan. I do the office, you do the calls and Roger works during the week to pay the bills."

"We're doing quite well with the recommendations from the Police. Even the surrounding Police Forces suggest us at times. Perhaps we can afford Roger to get more involved during the week."

Janine frowned at the thought. "It would help, but we don't know all the outgoings like taxes and such until the first year is over. "

"I suppose. You always were more sensible than me." Neil grinned at the girl he had known for many years, the sister of his dead best friend. They were both alone now and it seemed sensible that they stayed together. All three of them. Even Roger had nobody but them. Three young people who had taken on bureaucracy and won. It had given them the confidence to start the agency in order to help others.

The front door slammed which announced the arrival of Roger and the shopping.

"The supermarket was quite busy. It's a sure sign there are a lot of visitors here." Roger's voice came from the kitchen as he dumped the shopping on the worktop. "I brought pies from the butchers, he was just closing and glad to be rid of them, the fish and chip shop isn't open until later and I'm famished." Not having received any answer from the other two he came into the living room. "Something the matter?"

"Someone is coming to see us at seven thirty."

"A client?"

"Yes. He says it's urgent." Janine said.

"Who is he, a recommendation?"

"That's the problem." Neil cut in. "He never gave his name and he knows about us. He insisted we were all three here."

Roger looked at Janine and noted her tension. "Don't worry, we're both here."

"I wish we had a gun." Neil muttered.

"No!" Roger almost shouted. "I know in the army you were used to carrying a gun but in the outside world it is dangerous and illegal."

"I know." Neil said soothingly. "I just feel vulnerable sometimes, especially when Janine is worried."

"Well don't. Look on the bright side. Who knows, this could be our big break."

Janine laughed. "You are such an optimist, Roger."

"Well why not. We're doing OK. People are beginning to know about us and the work is much more regular now. Even the Police ask us to make enquiries for them sometimes. It can't get much better than that, surely. The next you know we'll all be enrolled as Special Constables and given uniforms.

"Heaven forbid!" Janine grimaced. "You wouldn't get me in one of those. Just because you fancied joining up."

"It would hardly apply to me. I do have a prison record, remember." Neil joked.

"Oh Neil. You don't, not any more. You were proved innocent."

"I'm only joking, Janine" But they all knew that his two years imprisonment and dishonourable discharge from the army still rankled, even though he had been exonerated. It was hard to forget when he drove every day in the car bought with his compensation.

At seven thirty sharp the doorbell rang and Janine went to answer it.

The room had been prepared. The coffee pot on the side cupboard was bubbling, a jug of milk and bowl of sugar sitting beside the cups and saucers. Mugs might be the order of the day in their home but in the office china cups and saucers gave a more professional image.

The man who followed her in was fairly tall, slim and slightly stooped. Around fifty years old he had that pale complexion of a dark haired man who spent all his time at a desk in an office pouring over dusty papers. He could have been mistaken for a solicitor's clerk except for the quality of the dark suit he was wearing.

Roger and Neil stood to meet him and indicated a comfortable chair.

Neil glanced at Roger and saw him thoughtfully analysing the man, so he began the interview.

"I understand you told Miss Mathers you needed to speak to all three of us. Could you explain why?"

The unnamed man looked between the three of them. "This is a very private and difficult matter which will require you all to be involved."

Roger spoke for the first time. "Who are you sir, and how do you know about us? You are not from this area."

The man smiled. "No. You are correct. I am a senior civil servant from a London Department of which you will be given no information. Suffice it to say the matter is urgent and every government minister and civil servant in London knows about you."

"So you work for the Ministry of Defence." Neil announced. "We were expecting them to try again to inflict retribution but presumed it would be a soldier not a clerk!"

The man stiffened. "I am not here for retribution." He frowned. "Has someone tried?"

"Let's just say a senior army officer with a very aggressive attitude visited Janine in her flat. Luckily, we had prepared for any eventuality. If we hadn't been available she would not have answered the bell."

"I will speak to someone about that." He rubbed the side of his face, he was obviously nervous. "One of our trusted clerks is missing and I need to you find him."

Roger and Neil glanced at each other. Neil was to continue to interview.

"Why us, Mr no name. If a clerk is missing it should be the London Police or the Security Service."

"It is not a Police matter and there is a possibility MI5 is involved."

"And you wish us to investigate MI5 on your behalf!"

The man cleared his throat, then stood and walked to the window. Outside his driver was leaning against the expensive car smoking a cigarette.

He took a deep breath. "I suppose it does sound strange. I just have this fear of saying too much. It is part of my lifelong training to say nothing because of the official secrets act, and yet I came to you because I thought you could find the truth. How can you do that if I don't trust you?" He turned and came to lean on the back of his chair. "My name is Walter Summers and I am the Private Secretary to Sir Amos Herbert, the chair of a very important and, I must stress, little known committee engaged in the defence of our country. Yes, it does include the heads of the services, MI5 and others I will not specify, but they know nothing of this investigation." He walked round the chair and sat, cleared his throat and requested another cup of coffee. Janine stood to pour it.

"Something is happening that I cannot disclose to you but enough to say that Sir Amos requested classified files from the archives of several years ago. He spent a great deal of time with each, then returned them, requesting another. I presumed he had whatever information he needed as he convened a meeting this coming Thursday, but last Friday morning he requested another file. He insisted it was not sent by courier as the information was too confidential, so I sent my assistant Percy Blenkinsop to fetch it on Friday afternoon. He often fetched items for us. He was due to leave on holiday that evening. He showed me the file and checked everything listed was in it, put it in the safe and locked it ready for Sir Amos on Monday morning." He hesitated.

Roger stood and went to pour himself another coffee and leaned against the cupboard. "Mr Summers, why do I get the feeling it is not Mr Blenkinsop you are missing?"

Summers fidgeted. "There were two letters missing from the file when the safe was opened this morning."

"And you believe Percy Blenkinsop took them?"

"It certainly looks that way, but Percy lives for his work, he has been honest to a fault for his whole working life. He checks everything, counts everything, never asks awkward questions. I find it hard to believe."

"Could anyone else have taken them?"

"I don't see how."

"Who has access to the safe?"

"There are three keys, Sir Amos has one, I have one and Percy has one. Sir Amos believes Percy came back after we left and took the letters."

"Was there any unpleasantness between them?"

"No. In fact recently Sir Amos has been very friendly with him. He says that is what has upset him most."

"Which leaves you, Mr Summers."

"It could ruin my career and lose me my pension for something I know nothing about."

"Is that why you came to us?" Janine asked.

"Partly." He was rubbing his cheek in nervousness. "Sir Amos suggested as we could not ask MI5, especially as Percy could be one of theirs, I should employ a

Private Investigator to find where Percy had gone." He was rubbing his cheek again. "If they could retrieve the documents then we could have the Investigator 'silenced'." Summers took a large gulp of his coffee.

"And you thought of us who could be 'silenced' with no questions asked, and everyone would be happy!" Said Roger, sarcastically.

"No, Mr Williams! Perhaps I know rather more of your previous exploits than you realise. The Army hierarchy wanted you eliminated but even MI5 refused. If anyone touched you the Army would always be the ones who would be blamed, whoever it was. It would have brought down the whole of the senior personnel of the Army and MI5 warned them. You were not touched because you came under the protection of MI5."

"Why?"

"Why, Mr Williams? Because you were extremely clever. You let nobody know how good your evidence was until you published it and gave it to the papers. At that point there was no way to refute anything. Apparently, someone tried to find the registration of your car in the hope of causing an accident which included all of you, but you had no car and seemed to be working alone. The public would have brought down the government if anything had happened to you. You are famous, and any accident to you will rebound on British bureaucracy. That's why I thought of you. You are untouchable. You squirrel out the truth and say nothing until you know the whole story."

"And who are we supposed to report to?"

Summers stared while he thought. It took some time. "How about – the Prime Minister?"

Roger laughed. "You understood what I was thinking."

"I did. Anyone from our department could hide the information. It could not be leaked to the press, so someone like the Prime Minister whose position depends on the public seems the only safe person."

"IF we take this commission who will be paying us?"

Summers looked surprised. "IF you take the case?"

"Indeed, Mr Summers. If. We need to discuss if we are all prepared to deal with this, especially as I still have other employment."

Summers put his hand in his pocket and withdrew a fat envelope. "This is the first payment of a thousand pounds, there will be the same again when you conclude. Perhaps you would like some time to discuss it. I will have my driver give me a tour of the sea front."

"Thank you, Mr Summers. Half an hour would be good, although I give you fair warning, we may have more questions when you return."

Summers nodded and rose from his chair. Neil saw him out.

CHAPTER TWO

he three stared at each other.

"Do we take it?" Janine looked between the two men.

"What do we know? A man goes on holiday and two letters go missing. How did he know they would be there that day? Was it a spur of the moment theft? From the way he describes him he sounds a real pleb, not someone who would act on the spur of the moment. We need to know about family, friends, where he goes and what his outside interests are. Surely the civil service has a file on everyone and where they come from." Roger mused.

"Would you take your office keys on holiday? Perhaps he left them at his room or flat and someone stole them." Neil was making notes in his book.

"If he is still alive. Perhaps someone removed him to get the keys."

Janine shivered.

"Do you want to take it?" Roger asked Neil.

Neil looked at his fingers. "It does sound rather more interesting than lost dogs."

Roger laughed. "I thought you looked interested. It would mean me giving up my job. It would need all three of us to be involved."

"I wish we had an Identity Card issued by the Police. I get no end of trouble because I look too young!"

"You need to get more lines on your face. I could give you a few!" Roger joked "If MI5 are our protectors, perhaps we can get an official card from someone. It's worth a try."

They all leaned back in their chairs searching for ideas.

"So, let's summarise." Roger said. "Where are his keys, where did he say he was going on holiday, has anyone checked, and was he alone? What did he do in his spare time and who was with him? What about his background?"

"Will Mr Summers sign one of our forms?" Janine asked.

"That's a good point. If not, we can hardly take his case. Would it be legal and what trouble could we be in if anyone questioned us? Not to mention where we got the thousand pounds from. They may think we're involved in some way." Roger looked over at Neil's notes.

"How can we make sure they don't think we're involved?" Neil queried.

"He has to sign a form and we want an official Identity Tag from someone to prove who we are."

"It will take some organising."

"True, but you're the best, Roger, and if you give up work we can both make enquiries while Janine co-ordinates here."

"So it all depends on Mr Walter Summers."

Summers was much less confident when he returned. He felt as if he were being inspected, no wonder these young men were so successful.

Janine placed an agreement in front of him.

"What is this?" He enquired.

"This is our standard agreement. I have added the cost as you described, half before and half after."

"Why do I need to sign this?"

"Because without it we have no legal status and no way to declare the thousand pounds." Roger answered.

"Ah. I suppose not. I must admit that had not occurred to me. In the circumstances I would not put you in jeopardy."

Neil visibly relaxed.

Roger leaned forward.

"Now Mr Summers. We will require all the details of Percy Blenkinsop that you have. A photograph, address, family background, all the things that the civil service usually keep. Plus, any known friends, any hobbies, not to mention what you know of where he said he was going on holiday."

Summers lifted his brief case and unlocked it, removing a folder. "I hope it is all here. As to where he was going on holiday, he said he was going to the south of England but not staying in one place. I presumed he was going walking and he never contradicted me."

"Was he going alone?"

"That he never said, although I had the impression he was meeting someone. He seemed almost excited, well as much as he ever was."

"Just one more thing. I wonder if you can help us. We are all young, and officials often don't believe who we are when we question them. We have asked the local Police to allow us an official identity badge of some kind, Inspector Dutton suggested it, but the Chief Constable in the area is new and has no knowledge of us."

"I doubt that. But in the circumstances, it will be better if you have some official identity. I will make arrangements."

"Thank you, it will be helpful."

For the rest of the evening none of them spoke, each shut in with his own thoughts. They barely said goodnight.

Breakfast saw them all alert.

"No more cases, Janine. We will no doubt be travelling around a great deal. How many are still outstanding?"

"Nothing urgent that I can't finish in the next few days, hopefully." Neil said.

"Then tonight we do a full plan of what we need to check. If you can go through the file and see where we need to visit, Janie. I'll give my notice today, although it will be the end of next week before I am totally free."

* * *

"Come in, Williams? Is there a problem?"

"Not as such, Mr Brant. But I need to give my notice."

"On a Tuesday morning!"

"I wanted to give you as long as possible, sir. I know I need to work to the end of next week."

"What brought this on so suddenly?"

"We have a case, sir. A very important one which needs all three of us."

"I had wondered how long before you would leave. I'll be sorry to lose you. You've been a steady worker and no trouble."

"Thank you, sir."

"Is it really important enough to give up your job completely? Could you not work part time?"

"No, sir. It needs us to be in London in particular. It's not local."

"A large company then?"

"A government department, sir." Roger murmured.

Mr Brant stared at him quietly.

"That is important."

"Yes sir."

"And you need to start as soon as possible?"

"Yes, Mr Brant."

"Then don't worry about your notice. Go home and someone will drop last week's pay packet in on Friday."

"Are you sure sir?"

"Get out before I change my mind, Roger." He held out his hand and Roger took it. "Good luck, lad."

"Thank you, sir."

The front door opening brought Neil and Janine into the hall.

"Roger! What's happened."

"Brant let me off without serving my notice."

"What did you tell him?" Neil frowned.

"We had a case from a Government Department."

"Ah."

"Well I never said which."

"We don't know which." Janine reminded him.

"So! A planning meeting?"

Neil lifted the large blackboard stored behind the cupboard and hung it on the hooks like a painting. On the left he wrote 'Questions' as a heading.

What happened to his safe key?

Did he tell his landlady where he was going?

Does she know who his friends are – who he met?

What time did he expect to leave – can we prove if he did

What does she know about him?

Does he have friends at work?

How often does he go home?

Does he write to his mother?

Does she know if he had any hobbies?

Does she know where he is?

Does Summers know more that he is saying and can we trust him?

"Where do we go first?" Neil amused.

"London to where he's been living. His landlady must know when he left and when he's due back, she may know more that we realise. They can be wily old birds, landladies. We should both go together, Neil, then if we get any leads we can split up to save time."

"Do we go in the car?"

"To begin with, yes. Then you'll be in a position to follow any leads outside London."

"His mother lives near Barnsley." Janine noted.

"That could be something for you to follow up. Your accent is more acceptable up there than mine." Roger laughed.

"What's wrong with my accent!"

"Joke, Neil. Did you never notice how the further north we went the less people trusted me and the more they trusted you. It's not your accent, it's mine. What cases do we have still needing to be finished?"

"Only the missing son, one." Janine said. "Neil was in Brighton yesterday."

"He's not on the voting register, but then he might not have been there for long enough."

"What did he do? I thought he worked for a precision engineering company."

"He did. Apparently he was quite skilled."

"So, are there any precision engineering companies along the south coast? There must be a register of some sort. Could you find that out, Janine."

"I told you we needed your brain." Neil muttered.

"There's nothing wrong with your brain, you just like driving around in your car too much."

"Find a list and we'll make some telephone calls to suitable companies. 'I understand you have a … working for you' type of call. If he is working there, we can arrange to drive over later and speak to him. We only need to give him the message. If he doesn't want to give us his address then so be it. At least we can tell the family where he is working and that he is well and not living on the streets."

"I'll start phoning directory enquiries. The sooner we start the sooner you can leave for London. I'll look for a small hotel near to where you need to be."

"You're a treasure, Janie." He grinned at her. "I'll go and make some coffee." He ducked out before Janine could pull a face at him.

Two days later Roger and Neil set off to drive to London, armed with their new identity cards, leaving Janine with a fully set up work board on which to note answers and any new questions, names of contacts and messages to be passed on. Once the two men parted she would be their point of contact.

Marny Hotel had probably once been a lodging house but was now renovated to offer washbasins in every room and a bathroom and toilet on both upstairs floors, with a small dining room that catered for breakfast and a very simple evening meal if required. The room was nothing special but it was adequate to their needs, they would be out most of the time, it was just somewhere to sleep and leave their suitcases.

A visit to a Smiths Newsagents furnished them with a map of London and a local map giving them a better understanding of distances in the area.

Stoat Lane was neither elegant nor downtrodden. In an area of tree lined roads of houses declaring their wealthy or at least middle class occupants, turning into Stoat Lane was something of a shock. Here were housed families with hopeful prospects or those sinking for lack of funds but unwilling to move from what they saw as an area where they belonged. No doubt there were others beside Mrs Bilton who took in lodgers to enable them to maintain their position in life. That must be why there were several elderly cars parked in the narrow street.

Neil was relieved they had left their obviously very new car on the wider road, it could have showed up the age of the few vehicles here.

Number 26 looked no different to any of the other houses with their brightly painted doors and well-scrubbed front steps. The fronts of these houses were deliberately well maintained giving a lie to any suggestion of poverty.

Roger knocked on the door while Neil looked around for twitching net curtains suggesting avenues for further investigation of Percy Blenkinsop's lifestyle.

Mrs Bilton opened the door and smiled in the hope that this was a possible lodger.

"Mrs Bilton. I wonder if we could have a word with you about your lodger Percy Blenkinsop? We have been asked to find information about someone who we believe Mr Blenkinsop knows."

"I'm afraid Percy is on holiday at the moment."

"So we have been told, but probably you can give us some help." Roger gave her his best smile. He had deliberately dressed in a good suit to impress her. Having lived in lodgings he understood how landladies assessed anyone arriving at their door who could be a potential lodger, and jeans and a polo sweater did not go down very well. He held up his very newly acquired identity card which she peered at.

"Oh, you're from Bournemouth. My cousin lives near Bournemouth, a lovely area. Do come in." She stepped back to allow them in.

"This is my colleague Mr Phelps, Mrs Bilton."

She looked slightly askance at Neil in his more relaxed outfit.

The front room was obviously meant for the use of her lodger. The chairs were comfortable but elderly and sported antimacassars and arm rests to keep them clean, showing that Mrs Bilton had either had a lodger or a husband in the distant pass whose hair oil needed to be guarded against.

There was a basic gas fire in the hearth and on one wall was a table with a lacy look tablecloth in easy wipe plastic. Either side of which were two upright chairs.

"Is Percy Blenkinsop your only lodger, Mrs Bilton?" Neil enquired.

"He is at the moment. I had another, Billy Norman, but he was killed in an accident almost three weeks ago."

"Did he work with Mr Blenkinsop?"

"Oh no. Billy was an accounts clerk. He worked in the garage on Alder Street. Such a shock it was. Fell under a bus during rush hour. They did say somebody had bumped him and over he went, but they never found who it was. Really upsetting it was and such a shame. They were both single and rather reserved, and they had really only just become friends."

Roger looked at Neil and raised his eyebrows.

"When you say friends, Mrs Bilton, did they go about together?"

"Only once or twice, just to the local pub, although neither of them was what you could call a drinker. Preferred a nice cup of tea, both of them."

"Was that Saturday nights?" Neil suggested.

"Oh no. Mr Blenkinsop was never here at weekends."

"Not ever!" Roger was surprised and intrigued.

"No. I think he might have gone to visit his mother occasionally, but I have no idea where he usually went."

"Did he ever take Mr Norman with him?"

"Only that last weekend, the one before he died."

"Mrs Bilton, how did you know he didn't go to his mother's every weekend?"

"Well he would say when he was. And his washing was different. He never had mud or grass on his things when he'd been home"

Neil frowned. He was writing furiously in his note book.

"And you say Mr Norman went with him the last weekend?"

Mrs Bilton frowned.

"Did he leave on a Saturday morning?"

"No, he came home Friday after work to fetch his suitcase and off he went in his car."

"He has a car?"

"Oh yes. The dark blue one outside."

"Did he not take it on holiday?"

"No. Everything was as normal, his suitcase was packed, he came home and I expected him to take his car but he said he was going by train. I saw him check he had his ticket before he left."

"Did he seem excited, was he going with friends?"

"I really don't know, he never said, but of course he was excited, he was going on holiday."

"And he was going for two weeks?"

"Yes. I said I would give his room a good clean while he was away. Why not ask him about his friend when he gets back?"

"We will, Mrs Bilton, but the matter is urgent and we need to find all his friends quickly. Are you sure you know of no other friends?"

"Definitely not! I don't pry, Mr Williams. I leave my lodgers to their privacy."

"Well thank you Mrs Bilton. If you should remember anything that could be of interest will you ring this number and leave a message with Miss

Mathers." Roger handed her their card and she looked closely at it.

"Oh, I see. There are three of you."

There are Mrs Bilton."

"Why do I know your names from somewhere?"

"Perhaps someone has mentioned us. Thank you for your time. We'll see ourselves out."

Standing in the street outside the closed door the two looked at each other.

"This is going to happen all the time. As soon as they read our names they remember us."

"Perhaps we shouldn't give out cards unless we need to. If we're working alone, one name won't be remembered. Perhaps we ought to get some business cards made with WMP Private Detective Agency and a telephone number. We could get it printed in the machine at the railway station."

"I said you were the brainy one." Neil grinned and patted him on the back. "Do we need to see anyone else? There's a very mobile net curtain across the road." He laughed.

"OK, why not. You can never have too much information." Roger grinned back.

They crossed the road and knocked on the door where the curtain was now very still. After a short time an elderly lady opened it a crack.

"Excuse me. Do you think we could have a word with you?" Roger handed her his identity card showing his name and face. She perused it as if she needed glasses.

"Do you need to fetch your glasses, Madam?" He asked.

"Well. Does it say Private something?"

"We are private investigators, Madam. We are talking to anyone who can help us and we wondered if you might have noticed anything interesting."

"What about?"

"The lodgers at number 26."

"Oh them!" She turned up her nose. "Full of herself is Mrs Bilton. So proud of her gentlemen being high powered civil servants, until one gets killed and we find he was a clerk in a garage."

"Can we come in?" Roger suggested.

"I suppose so. You are genuine, aren't you? Only I have no money and this is my son's house. He always tells me not to let anyone in but it gets boring sitting staring out of the window all day."

"I don't expect much happens down Stoat Lane." Neil suggested.

The old lady's eyes sparkled. "You'd be surprised, young man." She beckoned them into the front room and sat in a chair at the side of a table set in the bay window.

"You obviously take a great deal of interest in what happens outside."

"Well what else have I to do. Can't spend my whole life cleaning the house. Jim's hardly ever in these days. Got himself a regular girlfriend and don't want to bring her home to an old crone of a mother."

"So what can you tell us about number 26?" Roger asked, trying to steer her onto what they were there for.

"They both go to work regular and come back same every day. Never changes. You could set you watch by 'em. The one that's there now, he goes out at eight every morning and comes in at six almost on the dot."

"Every night? Does he go out later."

"Oh no. I never seen him go out except for twice when he went out with the other, that one that was killed. Except for Friday, of course. He never even has his dinner on a Friday. He's barely in the house for five minutes and then he's out with his suitcase and into his car. That's his the blue one."

"And did Mr Norman go with him at all?"

"Only the once. Perhaps he might have gone again if he was still alive. That's a bit funny you know."

"What is? Mrs... what is your name?"

"Mrs Garth, Amy Garth. Well there they were in the same house and hardly spoke according to her."

"Mrs Bilton?"

"Yes. Then they starts to get friendly and go down the pub a couple of times. He takes him for the weekend somewhere and then he's killed. Something funny going on there." She nodded to instil it into him.

"Did either of them have any visitors, Mrs Garth?" Neil realised getting information from her meant leading her away from her present thought.

"Never saw any. They hardly had post either, not until a couple of weeks ago when he waits outside the door while Posty comes down the whole road."

"That would be Mr Blenkinsop. Did you ask the postman about the letter?"

"What do you take me for!" Then her eyes sparkled. "Said it was official with a government stamp."

"Perhaps he was being promoted." Roger suggested.

"Posty thought it was a passport, it was the right size, he said."

"Thank you, Mrs Garth, you have been very helpful."

Neil was not that easily satisfied. "Mrs Garth, have you seen any strangers in the street, apart from us, that is?"

"Not recently. There was a car parked here for a couple of days. It was only there in the mornings and evenings. I thought someone was visiting but then I saw there was somebody sitting in it, like waiting."

"When did it leave. After Mr Blenkinsop went to work?"

"No, it was still there when Jim left just before eight thirty. I take the pots into the kitchen to wash up and it was gone when I came back."

"And it came back in the evening."

"Yes but it was only there for a couple of days."

"Was that before Mr Norman died?" Neil enquired.

Mrs Garth thought. "I don't remember seeing it afterwards, no."

"And you can think of nothing further that could be of interest."

"Well what is there of interest in this street. Now him over the road is on holiday all I see is her going for groceries, and there'll be pretty little of that with him away."

Getting out was a delicate business as Mrs Garth had someone to talk to and was not about to lose them too quickly. Eventually they extricated themselves and almost ran down Stoat Lane to the car.

"Well that was interesting and not at all what we were expecting." Roger mused. "I had thought Mrs Bilton would know more about his life but what she did say was not expected at all. Where did he go every weekend?"

"I'm worried about what happened to Billy Norman." Neil said, thoughtfully.

"Yes. So am I. We are told that Percy has disappeared and that MI5 could be involved. He makes friends with Billy, takes him on one of his weekends and days later he ends up dead." Roger mused. "It does sound suspect."

"And we still don't know where he went at weekends." Neil noted.

"His mother should know. Perhaps you should go up and ask her. I'll stay here and see if I can find anyone at his office who knows anything. I think I might look into this death. The local Police should be able to help there."

"You're better with the Police than I am. You talk their language." Neil grinned.

"Hardly! Still, they don't give me the willies like they do you." Roger grinned back. "Let's go and have those cards made without all our names on. I have a feeling Janie could be getting a few phone calls soon. If only to check who we are. I had hoped the official identity card would do that."

"Then can we get a decent meal before I leave. Small hotels may be cheap but the food leaves a lot to the digestion."

CHAPTER THREE

With a pocket full of newly printed personal cards containing his name, Roger Williams, Private Investigator, plus the office phone number, he arrived at the main Police Station for the district. He had presumed it would not be a local office.

The desk sergeant was fairly off hand, "Yes sir."

"Can you tell me if the death of Billy Norman was dealt with by this station?"

"And why would you be wanting to know that, sir?"

Roger gave him a serious stare. "What is that to you? Do you make the decisions for the whole of the area? I wish to know who was the investigating officer and if you will not help me then I will go to Scotland Yard and ask them, Sergeant …" Roger leaned over the desk to read his name badge … "Chorley."

The sergeant stiffened. "I was only checking, sir. No need to take that attitude. As it happened it was on our patch."

"May I please speak to whoever was the investigating officer?" He produced his official badge with his photograph.

"Oh, a Private Dick. Well I'll see if he is in, sir, if you would like to take a seat while I enquire."

Roger went nowhere, he was not going to allow him to say things on the phone that he couldn't hear.

Detective Inspector Harwood was discussing a case with Detective Sergeant Parry when the phone rang. Parry answered it.

"There's a private investigator here wants to talk about the Norman case."

"What is there to talk about, the man fell under a bus."

"We can't be sure he wasn't pushed, sir. This fellow may have information."

"Send him up then."

It was a bored Inspector who turned to face the young man who entered his office.

"I thought you were a Private Dick!"

"I am a Private investigator, Inspector." He pulled out his official card again and showed him.

Harwood frowned. "You're very young, what are you..."

"A Private Investigator." Roger answered firmly. How old he was had no bearing on anything. "Is the case still open?"

"No. The man fell under a bus and there's no family or anyone who can help, unless you can."

"I thought there was a report of someone pushing him? That's what the paper said."

"Well, pushed, knocked, what's the difference?"

"Have you found him?"

"Who?"

"The man you were looking for who knocked or pushed him. The report thought he was a local drunk. Have you found him?"

"No. He obviously scarpered when he realised what had happened."

"Scarpered because he was frightened or scarpered because he had been told to? Drunks don't usually move somewhere strange even supposing he could remember what happened."

"Who would have told him to?"

"That depends on if you have found his body. Have you put out an APB on him. I doubt he would be found in this area, they would take him away to where nobody knew him. Just a drunk who died of drink or fell into a pond or lay forgotten in a derelict hut."

Harwood sat up straight and frowned.

"What do you know and why come now?"

"This is not the case I am working on but it has intruded on it and could have some connection. I need to know if a body has been found and where. It could give me the direction I need."

"What case are you working on that the Police don't know about?"

"I can't tell you."

"Can't or won't."

"Can't! If you went to Scotland Yard and had me arrested, I still couldn't tell you about my case. I don't have to satisfy the press like you do, so I get cases that need more privacy. I suggest you think about it, Inspector. It could make or break your career."

He took his new card out of his pocked.

"If you find anything, please phone this number."

Roger left the station appearing calm and confident. Inside he was suffering from shock. 'Bloody hell, did I just ball out a DI.' No doubt there would be fall out from this.

In the office Harwood was angry.

"Who the hell does he think he is. Where was he from, did his badge say?"

"The badge was issued by Bournemouth, sir." Parry had taken special note.

"Then phone Bournemouth Police and find out who he is and why he thinks he can come here telling me my job."

"He does have a point, sir. We haven't made any effort to find the man."

"Will he even remember, Parry. They said he was a local drunk. Now he is a local to somewhere else."

Roger went back to the hotel in frustration. From his assessment of the Inspector he doubted anything would be done. If the drunk was found it could give him some indication of where Blenkinsop went, or who he knew. The best he could do was try to infiltrate the civil servants who worked in the same building as

Percy. Perhaps he had friends there who would know something of where he went at weekends, which now seemed to hold the key to what had happened.

* * *

Neil Phelps drove north and the further he went the worse the weather was. This was supposed to be summer. He found a cheap bed and breakfast close to a decent looking restaurant for an evening meal and thought about settling down for the night. A few enquiries and a local map gave him some idea of where Mrs Blenkinsop lived and he was grateful he had a car as it was in a quiet rural area. He wondered how Percy had gone to work in Barnsley Town Hall, was there a bus or did he cycle? Or did he already have his car? They should have taken note of the car registration number.

He stopped several times to check the map before he found it. A row of houses on a quiet road overlooking fields and the river. No wonder Percy was a quiet self-contained person, brought up in a place like this.

There was no answer when he knocked. Perhaps she was deaf and couldn't hear. He knocked again. Perhaps she was out shopping or never answered the door in the evening. Neil went and sat in his car to wait. It was boring and the day had been tiring and his concentration slipped as he drifted.

The knock on the car window started him awake. He wound it down.

"What are you doing!" An elderly woman was staring accusingly at him.

"Are you Mrs Blenkinsop?" He stammered.

"No. What do you want with her?"

"I need to speak to her." He fumbled to take out his official identity card.

The woman stared at it. "What's the matter. Is it Percy?"

"I need to talk to her. Do you know where she is?"

"She's gone to visit her sister in Worksop."

"Do you know the address or phone number?"

"No."

"This is important. How can I contact her?"

"I don't know."

"Do you know her sister's name."

"Mary, that's all I know."

"Will any of the other neighbours know?"

"I doubt it, she's a very private person. Is it Percy?"

"Not directly." Neil lied. "But we need to know something which she might be able to tell us."

"Percy's gone on holiday, hasn't he? That's why you're here."

"Yes. How can I get in touch with his mother?"

"I'm sorry, I really don't know."

"Might she be back tomorrow?"

"She didn't say how long she was staying. You could come back and see."

"Thanks. I will." Neil wound up the window and started the car. Well this looked like it was going to be a wasted journey. He thumped the steering wheel in frustration. He would phone Janine and she would tell Roger, but there must be something he could do to find out about Percy's past. Would anyone at Barnsley Town Hall remember him? It was worth a try, although it was too late today. At least he could have a decent meal and a good night's sleep.

* * *

The morning saw Roger dressed to look like a middle rank civil servant as he made his way to where everyone was entering the anonymous building. He leaned on the architrave outside as if waiting for someone and pretended to read a newspaper, but he noted everything that happened. There was someone inside who nodded to people as they arrived but nobody showed their pass. Perhaps he could get in easily, but where would he go after that? He needed to find the canteen, there was bound to be one.

Where were the canteen supplies delivered? Somewhere round the back, he expected. After a long tour of the area he realised everything arrived by van which had a pass to get into the underground car park. Damn. Roger took himself to a local café to think things through.

"Another coffee, sir?" Roger looked up at the man behind the desk.

"Oh, yes. That would be good, thank you."

"You look troubled, sir."

"I'm looking for a friend of mine who works in an office near here but I don't know which department and I can't get in because I don't have a pass."

"Civil servant is he?" The man laughed. "They do like to pretend they're important even though they work for us."

"Yes. I don't want to make a fool of myself by going in asking questions, I might be arrested and I'm not a hundred percent sure it is that office building."

"Well if you stay here he may come to you. They come most lunchtimes. I sometime wonder what the food is like in their canteen that they come and eat sandwiches and pies from me."

"Perhaps it's the coffee, it is particularly good."

The man grinned. "Thank you, sir. I have been told that before."

Roger settled in a corner with his coffee and read his newspaper.

At just after twelve the first people started to arrive and Roger looked for someone who might be helpful. One man came over the speak to him.

"Hi. Toby said you were looking for your friend."

"Yes. Percy Blenkinsop, do you know him?" The young man frowned and shook his head. "There's a lot of us work there. Try someone else, you might get lucky."

Half an hour later more arrived, talking among themselves. It took until one fifteen before he found someone who knew Percy Blenkinsop.

"He's on holiday."

"Oh that's unfortunate. He never told me. I don't get up to London very often and was hoping to see him. Do you know where he's gone?"

"No. You know Percy, never tells anyone anything."

"That's true. Do you meet him at weekends?"

"Never see him outside the office. Nobody does. Someone did say they'd seen him having lunch with a girl from archives, but I've never seen them."

"Thanks. I'll get in touch when he gets back, although I won't be in London then." He grinned what he hoped was a nonchalant grin and the man left.

Nobody much knew him and he never came in here. So where else would he go, this was the only café near to the office. For the rest of the afternoon he walked around the area until his feet ached. He found a small café on the corner of a side alley, fell into a chair overlooking the main road and sat nursing a tea of indifferent flavour. He stared out of the window.

"You're not a courier?" The man wiping tables said.

"Courier? Courier for who?"

"You look like a civil servant but we don't get many here unless they're fetching something special from the archives." He nodded towards the large building on the opposite side of the road.

"The archives? Oh, you mean where they keep closed files."

"We're not supposed to know, of course."

"Do you get many in here for lunch?"

"Quite a few. It's the only time we're busy."

Roger took a sip of his tea and knew why only a few were regulars here.

"I'm in London and I was hoping to meet my friend but it appears he's gone on holiday. I think he used to meet a girl from the archives sometimes."

"There are one or two of those. Mostly the men are not so young and the girls are being given 'the wife doesn't understand me' routine."

Roger watched until they started to leave work and crossed the road to be nearer. He had to remember Percy was a quiet and private person so he would hardly meet a vibrant scintillating young lady, if any of them were. She would need to be as private as him.

Once everyone had left, he stayed until the stragglers wandered out. One or two of the girls might be of interest. One of them had to know Percy because he went to fetch files.

Tomorrow he would … Tomorrow was Saturday. Bother. Unless some of them worked on Saturday?

After his indifferent meal, he phoned Janine and gave her the information he had. Neil had not phoned which probably meant he was in a restaurant somewhere eating. She would phone through to him if there was any news.

* * *

Neil's visit to the Town Hall was less fraught than he had expected. Percy was still remembered as a good worker with no black marks against him, but they could give him no information of his hobbies or the whereabouts of his aunt in Worksop.

The area was full of school children acquiring their uniforms ready for school. Now that was a thought. Which school had Percy Blenkinsop attended and did anyone know who his friends were. Surely some of them were still living in the area.

The senior school was not open, although there were office staff there preparing for the new term. If he came in on Monday they would see if any of the older teachers could remember him. School had not started so he wouldn't be interrupting lessons.

What was he supposed to do until Monday? No doubt Roger would have had ideas. Why stay here when there was a bed for him at the Marly Hotel in London. It was only the middle of the afternoon so he had plenty of time.

* * *

Detective Sergeant Parry was once again arguing with Detective Inspector Harwood. Gently, of course, he wanted to keep his job.

"Should we not give the old lady some protection. After all it is only from her house anyone could see there were five of them. The gang would know who had given them the information."

"You think they're going to risk going there again?"

"Yes. I do, sir. This isn't a gentle burglary, it's a violent gang of young men. How would it look if something happened to her and we hadn't protected her? At least suggest she go to visit someone. Once the papers report it was five young men, I don't give her much of a chance."

Harwood stared at him. "You get very belligerent sometimes, Parry."

"Yes, sir. Well I was told about cases where we were too late."

"Such as?"

"That Army case for one. They gave all the information to the Police together with a list of informants who needed protection before they gave the story to the papers."

"I think that case has caused us to rethink a great deal. The problem was that nobody took them seriously. Well, would you. A damaged girl, Mathers wasn't it, frightened of anyone touching her and a disgraced and angry soldier. I doubt I would have even read the book."

"No, sir. I can assure you, you wouldn't have." Parry muttered.

"Is that sarcasm, Parry."

"Not as such, just a little home truth. I know you always said they were not capable of doing it for themselves."

"I'm not saying the interviews by Phelps were not genuine, but he was an emotional mess. Someone had to be the mastermind behind it."

"Would you have listened if the mastermind had told you."

"Of course I would."

"I doubt it, sir."

"What has got into you, Parry?"

"You know that Private Investigator who came last night?"

"Did you contact Bournemouth?"

"Yes sir. They did give them the Identity Cards. Apparently, the Chief Constable was being slow and suddenly he was told to issue them immediately. The instruction came from London."

Inspector Harwood looked up suddenly. "Who in London?"

"Nobody said. But I think the company he works for might be of interest. They opened six months ago and are called Williams, Mathers and Phelps, sir. You know that mastermind you wanted to meet? Well I think yesterday you did."

Parry decided it was time for a coffee and left before Harwood said anything.

Before the day was out a full description of the drunk was circulated to all areas asking to be sure to check all dead bodies.

CHAPTER FOUR

Roger had already eaten when Neil arrived unexpectedly. He was forced to sit and watch him eat a far superior meal to his.

Apart from exchanging information there was little else they could do. Everything was tied to enquiries when people were at work. It was frustrating that they had no idea where Percy Blenkinsop had gone on his weekends, here they were wasting theirs with nothing to investigate.

They did go to the archives and watch for who was working on a Saturday, but there was no suitable young lady to be seen, so they spent their time seeing the sights, walking in parks and visiting Battersea Fun Fair, where Roger spent some hard earned money on visiting a fortune teller, much to the scorn of Neil. He emerged with a smile on his face and was not to be upset no matter what Neil said.

Early Monday morning they started the investigations again, Neil driving up to Barnsley and

Roger taking his newspaper to watch for a suitable girl from the archives.

For the second day Roger waited outside the building. It was a long shot but she was exactly what he had imagined and she only had to say no.

Today she was dressed in the same brown coat and flat heeled shoes and wore a paisley headscarf. Again, she made for the same café and sat in the same corner.

Roger approached with a smile. "Hello. You look lonely, do you mind if I join you? I suppose you are normally with Percy?"

The girl looked up in surprise. "Oh, do you know Percy?"

"Not very well I have to admit, but I have seen you together before."

The girl blushed. "He's not my boyfriend. We're just friends but we do meet for lunch sometimes."

"So he never suggested you go on holiday with him?"

"Of course not! In any case he'd been invited by someone so he could hardly arrive with me in tow."

"I understand he's gone walking. Do you like walking?"

"Has he? He never said exactly where he was going."

"Just to the south coast." Roger prompted.

"Yes."

"Did you know he was going before you saw him on Friday afternoon?"

"Not really, he just mentioned that he would be away for a couple of weeks on holiday. I think it must have been arranged very recently." She looked up rather worried. "How do you know I saw him on Friday? Who are you?"

"I could ask you the same. My name is Roger Williams and I can't tell you what I do, the same as you can't tell me what you do. But I do know he came to fetch a file on Friday afternoon."

"That's true. Mavis Frost." She said and held out her hand which Roger shook. "Do you work in the area?"

"No, I only come to London when the boss sends me for a special reason."

"Oh, I see." She sounded rather upset. Perhaps she thought her luck had changed.

"Percy didn't really say much about you. He is a very careful person, isn't he?"

"I don't mind that. If I give him a file he always checks it again before he signs for it, but it isn't because he mistrusts anyone, he is just like that, very careful." She looked shocked at what she had just said.

"It's OK. I know about him fetching the file. His boss mentioned it."

"You know his boss?"

"Summers, yes."

"Oh, I thought you meant . . ."

"I know who you thought, but he never told me. Best if you don't tell anyone. Probably Summers shouldn't have mentioned it."

"Oh I won't say anything. It might get me into trouble."

"I doubt you have done anything wrong." He smiled at her.

"But I shouldn't have talked about it."

"You didn't, I did." Roger assured her.

"That's true. You won't tell anyone will you."

"No, I won't tell anyone."

"I need to get back. It was nice meeting you, Roger."

"It was nice meeting you Mavis."

Roger watched her leave the café then took out his notebook and wrote her name and everything she had confirmed.

That was the last connection he had and she could tell him nothing. He hoped Neil could find out something.

Neil phoned directly to the Marly Hotel that evening, he sounded excited.

"Roger you'll never guess what I've found out. Percy and his friends used to play about in a boat when they were young. He was always intense and spent his time reading about how to sail it properly, ordering them about. He was quite hooked on it. The school friend I met thought he might have joined a sailing club. That would account for the mud and grass stains. I can't find which as his mother is away and nobody knows her sister's address."

"Brilliant! But where he goes is still a problem. Are you coming back here?"

"Yes, but not until the morning. Have you spoken to Janine?"

"Not since last night, why?"

"I've been trying to phone her but she isn't answering."

"I'll try. It could just be a problem with the phone lines."

Roger fished out his money to put in the phone box and began to dial.

"Mr Williams?" A voice said behind him.

He turned to see two men standing close to him.

"Will you come with us, please." It wasn't a question.

"No. Why? Who are you?"

He was given no answer but was propelled out of the hotel foyer and pushed into a car with blacked out windows. The desk clerk was staring in horror.

* * *

The doorbell was rung with some force and was followed by hammering on the door. Janine was alone and rather nervous of opening it so she closed the security chain and turned the handle to open the door a crack.

"Phelps!"

A rough looking man had his face to the crack in the door.

"Open the door!" He shouted.

"Mr Phelps is not here at the moment." Janine was trying to sound calm while inside she was shaking.

"Let me in, Bitch!"

"Mr Phelps is not here, sir. He is in the north of England."

"You're lying. Open this door or I will."

Janine tried to push the door the small amount in order to turn the key but he stepped back and threw his shoulder at the door, once, twice and the screws gave, driving the door inward and knocking Janine to the ground. She screamed, but she was alone and it would not be heard by anyone from any of the neighbouring houses.

He was tall and broad and carried himself with confidence even though he was unshaven and slovenly dressed.

He dragged Janine by the arm into the office and threw her across the room.

"Where is he!"

"I told you, he is in the north of England making enquiries."

"Liar! He's in the house! Open the house door!" He stepped towards her and slapped her face, knocking her head to one side. As the fell she caught the table and the telephone wire, pulling the phone with her. As she heard the buzzing she put our her hand and dialled 999 while covering the sound by screaming, before struggling to her feet. The man was searching the room.

"Where's the key to the house door!" He shouted.

Janine shook. The last thing she wanted was for him to get into her house, she would never feel safe there again.

"We are Private Investigators, you saw the name on the door, Williams, Mathers and Phelps of Bournemouth." She said loudly, "Mr Phelps is in the north making enquiries." She could only hope the person on the other end of the phone line would realise she was in trouble.

He stood there facing her with a gun in his hand. **"The door to the house, NOW!"**

With trembling hands, she indicated the desk drawer. She put her hand inside to find the key and felt the pepper spray she had been advised to carry.

Janine held out the key with her hand and, as he leaned towards her to take it, she sprayed the pepper in his face and threw herself behind the desk. The gun fired twice, but he dropped it as he clawed at his face. Inspector Dutton's training came in as she stepped forward and kicked his shins until he dropped to the floor, when she kicked him between the legs, all the time shouting 'HELP, SEND HELP'. As he rolled around on the floor screaming, she picked up the gun as if it were hot and fled out of the front door still screaming for help.

A car was pulled up in the entrance to the drive and two men were getting out, who she presumed were friends of her attacker.

In panic Janine waved the gun at them.

They held up their hands palm first to calm her, but she was too frightened they would take the gun and shoot her. She hurled it into the overgrown shrubs where it sank among the branches and disappeared.

One of them went towards the house, the other took Janine by the arms, and in sheer terror she blacked out.

∗ ∗ ∗

Roger struggled to hide his intense fear. He had no idea where he was and there were no windows and only the door through which he had been pushed. Had this been where Blenkinsop had been brought?

There was a table and several upright chairs. He tried the door but it was locked. He worried how long he would be kept here before something happened to him. He must try not let them know he was afraid, he knew that would give them leverage over him. Should he pretend to know nothing or would they already know who he was. They had been at the hotel waiting so they probably knew why he was in London, but who had told them?

And who was 'them'. Just because Summers had thought MI5 might be involved, there was no guarantee they were his present captors. He was only relieved that Neil was in the north and not expected to join him until tomorrow. If Janine did not hear from him she would telephone the hotel and be told what had happened and inform Neil when he phoned in.

When the door opened it admitted three people. One was tall and thin and very serious, one appeared to be a guard as he took a chair and sat to one side staring intently at him, the third being small and rotund with a smiling face and carrying a tray of what smelled like coffee.

"Well now Mr Williams, I expect you would welcome a coffee." The small man noted. "Milk and sugar, or are you a cream man?" He joked. "Possibly not. Very few take cream these days."

Roger stared at them. This was a good cop bad cop routine.

The rotund man poured coffee and handed it to him.

"I've put sugar in to compensate for the shock you must be feeling. Biscuit?" He enquired holding out a plate. Roger still stared at him.

"I think he must be rather more shocked than I thought, Lionel."

The tall thin man rumbled to life. "I don't think so. I think he is working out how to deal with this and how much to tell us." He moved to the front of the desk and perched on it. "Now, Mr Roger Williams, Private Investigator, what are you investigating?"

Roger said nothing.

"Leave him to drink his coffee, Lionel." They both retreated to behind the table and drank coffee like it was an informal coffee morning. Roger's head spun. Perhaps he needed to take the initiative and shock them.

"Are you going to kill me like you killed Percy Blenkinsop and Billy Norman?"

Both of them looked totally bemused. Hardened criminals weren't supposed to do that.

"Who is Percy Blenkinsop and who is Billy Norman?" The one called Lionel asked.

Well that was a surprise. Of course, it depended on who they were. Perhaps if he asked the questions.

"Who are you and why have you dragged me here?"

"Dragged, Mr Williams. Were you not asked politely to accompany them? Tut, tut, I must have a word with them. As to who we are I would have expected you to know."

"Why?"

"Mr Williams, you have been seen loitering in front of government buildings and asking questions about people who work there. Did you think nobody would inform us?"

Roger stared at his hands. "Not as good as I thought, then."

Lionel laughed.

"Not bad, Mr Williams, but not good enough. Now do you know who we are."

"MI5"

"So perhaps you could tell me what you are doing and why."

"Well actually, no. I was told you could be involved."

"What does that mean?"

"It means that Percy Blenkinsop could be one of your men."

Lionel looked at his partner in surprise. "Now there's a new one for the book. Do I take it this Blenkinsop is a civil servant?"

"Yes."

"Ah. Something untoward seems to be happening here. Of course we know who you are, Mr Williams, you are alive because we have issued threats to your enemies. What we do not understand is why you have suddenly left your haven in Bournemouth and arrived on our doorstep."

There was a scuffle outside the door and someone crying. The guard stood up and opened the door. Someone entered trying to support an almost unconscious woman.

"Janine!" Roger shouted.

Janine lifted her head and seeing Roger threw herself at him, gripping his lapels and burying her face in his chest while fighting for breath. Gradually Roger closed his arms around her, holding her gently. How long had he dreamed of doing just this. Ever since he had carried her unconscious out of the sea she had never let him so much as touch her hand. Perhaps the fortune teller at Battersea Fun Fair had been right. If so, his future could be brighter than he had thought.

"It's all right, Janie. No one will hurt you." He stroked her hair as he supported her. Gradually she calmed and stopped fighting for breath. She pushed away from him in shock.

"Let go of me!"

"Janine, you came to me. Don't get so upset. Come and sit down."

Janine looked up at him not really realising what was happening but took the chair close to him.

"These appear to be MI5 if what they say is true." Roger joked with her.

"They came to kill me." Janine whispered.

"Kill you!" He turned to Lionel. "Did you send someone to kill her?"

"We sent a car to fetch her." He faced Janine. "Now tell me why you think we wanted to kill you."

Janine was having trouble breathing again because of her distress.

"Calm down, Janie. What happened?"

"He broke the door down and wanted to get into the house. He wanted Neil. He tried to shoot me. Then two men came and took me away. I don't remember much else."

"Do we have any information about this, Lionel. Would you like me to find out?"

"I think we should. I trust my men and I don't like the thought they could have their own agenda."

The smaller man left with a frown on his face.

"Would you like some coffee, Miss Mathers, hopefully it is still hot?" He poured a cup and looked to Roger to take it and add whatever sugar she liked.

"Here, Janine. What happened on the way here? Did they ask many questions?"

"I don't remember an awful lot. One of them tried to ask me things but I was so upset and whenever he took hold of my arm I think I lost consciousness."

Roger faced Lionel. "You do realise you have undone all the good work we have put in to make Janine more confident with men."

Lionel sat thoughtfully. "Sometimes we forget the effects of the damage, and we seem not to have known how fragile Miss Mathers is. People will be notified." He looked at Janine. "I must apologise, Miss Mathers. Sometimes we give out instructions without reading through the file sufficiently. You were only supposed to be brought here for a meeting."

The small rotund man came back in but he was not smiling.

"Apparently one of our operatives phoned the local police about an attack but they already knew. Someone had broken the safety chain to get in and had tried to shoot her. She was carrying the gun by the barrel when our boys turned up. She did a good job of disabling him, I think he needed hospitalization. We left him tied up, but it appeared she had managed to phone the police and they were already on their way. Our boys left before they arrived, but they did tell them where she had thrown the gun."

"No doubt the local Police will find out who he is."

"If he was asking for Neil then he could be army." Roger surmised.

"He will be dealt with, Mr Williams, have no doubt about that. It appears we arrived in the nick of time, or slightly too late. The two men in the car were not in any way connected to the man in the house. In fact, one of my men restrained him to make sure he did not leave before the Police arrived."

"Restrained?"

"Don't ask, Mr Williams. Now, is one of you going to tell me what this case of yours is all about?"

"We can't do that!" Janine blurted out, then sank back in her chair."

"Perhaps we need to make a few enquiries before we continue this conversation. We will take you to rooms where you can sleep and you will be given a meal. Perhaps that will calm both of you. You are not prisoners but I wish to keep hold of you until tomorrow when I have found out what we know of your dead men." Lionel almost smiled and the small man bustled them out into a lift.

"My name is Duncan and if you need anything you can ask me. But I am a fully paid up member, not a waiter. I say that because people often don't realise and it can cause embarrassment." He chattered on as he steered them into a suite of rooms. "This room is where you will be fed and if we continue down here, this is the bathroom and these are your rooms, choose whichever you wish. When you are calmer and settled, do come and let me know what you would like for dinner, or supper, whatever you wish to call it."

Duncan bustled out, leaving them staring at each other.

CHAPTER FIVE

ionel and Duncan tried to encourage them to talk but they were both too careful. Janine was tired and upset after such a harrowing day and excused herself to retire early. Roger only wished he could go and comfort her when he heard her crying during the night. He certainly did not trust any of the MI5 men, especially as he had no idea who had inflicted the fast developing bruise on Janine's face.

On the Wednesday morning they were given breakfast and left to themselves. Roger wondered if they hoped they would talk between themselves and if the room was bugged. He tried to make small talk about their home and what needed to be done to make it more comfortable and how to advertise the agency.

Eventually they ran out of innocuous things to discuss.

Janine and Roger were ensconced in deep comfortable chairs in the meeting room where everything seemed to happen, both of them deep in thought, when Neil appeared.

"They found you as well, did they?" Roger growled.

"Have you said anything?" Neil looked shaken. He dropped into a comfortable chair.

"Of course not. I accused them over the death of Percy Blenkinsop and Billy Norman."

Neil started in surprise. "What did they say?"

"They went away to check who I was talking about."

"They wanted me to tell them why we were in London. I told them I wasn't, I'd been up north so why accuse me? I thought I'd be in trouble but the plump one burst out laughing."

"But you said nothing?" Roger checked.

"Of course not."

"As they know about Percy and Billy, then we have been asked to check Percy is OK after Billy died. Simple as that. What else is there to tell." Roger looked around the room.

Neil looked at Roger and grinned then looked around wondering if their conversation was being monitored.

"So, where do we go if they let us leave here."

Neil looked directly at Janine. "I have an appointment this afternoon, if they let us out."

Janine suddenly looked stricken. "Oh God. I forgot."

"Don't worry, I got the call and made an appointment, although that was before the MI5 heavies brought me here."

Janine mouthed 'Summers' to Roger.

"Then we go home. There's nothing else for us in London. We have no further contacts and these lot appear to want us out of their hair." Roger had his eyebrows raised to indicate it had been said in case anyone was listening.

"We need to take Janine home and obviously she can't be left alone until we know exactly what happened. No doubt Inspector Dutton will come calling when he knows we are back." Neil grinned at her.

The door opened suddenly and Duncan arrived with a plate full of sandwiches, followed by Lionel.

"I suppose you want to eat before you leave."

"Are we going?" Roger asked.

"I'll bring you a pot of tea and coffee." He bustled out, returning after a minute or two with a laden tray and began to pour.

"I thought you might like to know the result of our enquiries." Lionel intoned. "The civil servant by the name of Percy Blenkinsop is on annual leave in the south of England and the fact that Billy Norman lived at the same lodgings was irrelevant to his falling under a bus. The case is closed and there is no indication that Blenkinsop is not alive and enjoying his holiday. No doubt he will return at the weekend and confound you all. You still have not told us why you started this search in the first place, but then Private Investigators are notorious at protecting their sources, however misleading they are. It is possible this is an elaborate hoax set up by someone you upset."

Roger kept his eyes down to avoid him guessing how far from the truth he was. Janine looked angry and

Neil's jaw had dropped. Roger only hoped he would not give anything away by taking a swing at him. Nobody belittled Neil and walked away unscathed. But perhaps Lionel was trying to wind him up enough to make him slip up.

Neil put down his plate and cup and stood up. "Can I go now or do you wish to continue insulting us."

Roger looked closely at Neil and realised he was in control. Perhaps this appointment with Summers was imminent and he wanted to leave quickly.

"Perhaps it would be best if we all go. I need to pick up my suitcase from Marly Hotel before we drive home, I can do that while you meet your friend."

Duncan looked rather askance at the wasted sandwiches but escorted them down through lifts and corridors, more than needed, Roger surmised, probably to confuse them. They emerged into an underground car park and were put in a taxi which drove them back to the Marly Hotel.

"So, where are we meeting Summers?" Roger asked.

"At a nice quiet little restaurant where we can get a meal as we never ate the sandwiches. So that if anyone is following us it won't look strange. Two o'clock."

"We need to get moving then."

"I don't expect to be able to park so we need a taxi. I'll ask the front of house to wave one down."

"It's a Hotel not a theatre, Neil."

Neil just grinned and they heard him pounding down the stairs.

They arrived early and ordered food. Both Roger and Neil ordered the roast chicken from the rotisserie, with chips, but Janine was still jumpy and not really hungry and decided just a jacket potato with cheese and coleslaw.

At two o'clock exactly Summers arrived and took a chair at their table.

"I thought you wanted no contact, Mr Summers?" Roger began.

"I did. But there has been a development, and it is my fault. You see, I was so worried I could be thought involved that I never really remembered what happened that evening. It was when I needed to open the small drawer I keep locked that I found his keys. After Blenkinsop had locked the safe he gave me the keys. He said it was safer to leave them with me than to leave them at his lodgings. I am so sorry, I seem to have caused you a great deal of trouble for nothing. It does, of course, beg the question of how anyone did get in. Unless there is a fourth key."

Roger put his head in his hands and Neil leaned back and groaned.

"It was the first question on our list, as well. What happened to his keys?" Roger shook he head.

"I was so upset that morning I never remembered locking them away, especially as Sir Amos had immediately suspected him. How will you continue with your enquiries? I imagine they have all been based around Blenkinsop."

"Who we have still not found, Mr Summers. If he arrives for work on Monday morning I imagine Sir Amos will instantly accuse him. What then?"

"I really don't know. Someone else must have a key. Someone we don't know about."

"If so, they are probably civil servants in that building, and MI5 have just warned us off."

"What!"

"We have been noted, well I have, asking questions and being around government buildings. They believe they have sent us home with our tails between our legs, Mr Summers. They obviously don't know us as well as they think. Although where we go from here is a problem. If you acquire any information please will you let us know, for right now you have just pulled the rug from under our feet where this investigation is concerned."

Summers never stayed and none of them finished their food.

Roger paid the bill while Neil flagged down a cab and they went silently back to the Hotel to pack his suitcase and pick up the car.

Evening saw them in their house suffering from silent depression. With no fresh food in the house, Neil drove Janine to the supermarket to stock up while Roger went through all the information they had, and made notes for a discussion when any of them could face it.

Thursday morning and all of them were avoiding talking about the problem. Neil phoned Inspector Dutton to tell him they were all home and Janine was safe. Within an hour he arrived with his sergeant, both eager to hear exactly what had happened.

"He broke the chain?" Dutton asked. "Perhaps you need a voice intercom instead. How did you manage to phone?"

"He dragged me in here to look for Neil and he hit me across the face."

"I wondered where that bruise came from." Roger worried. "I thought one of MI5 had hit you."

"I fell when he hit me and it dragged the phone onto the floor. When I heard the buzzing I realised I could dial 999. He wanted the key to get into the house."

"Oh no! That's the last thing you needed." Neil exclaimed as the extent of the ramifications sunk in.

"I felt horrified and angry, that's why I had the nerve to spray the pepper in his face."

"You did more than that." Dutton grinned.

"Well you had me trained how to protect myself, so I did. I think I left him in a lot of pain."

Dutton laughed. "Oh, you did that, all right."

"Well he intended to shoot me!"

"The emergency people heard the shots. It was pandemonium when the message came through. We expected to find you dead or wounded, instead we found a neat little package in a great deal of pain, just waiting for us to pick him up."

"How did they leave him, the MI5 blokes?" Roger asked.

"A work of art, really. Crouching position with his head forward and tied into a parcel with his own belt. He's still in hospital. I won't ask just how hard you kicked him because we can't know what MI5 did, but he is certainly not going to walk for quite a time and I doubt he will father any children."

"Who is he?" Neil asked.

"Someone you know rather well. A certain army prison officer who spent his time causing as much hurt and unpleasantness to his inmates as he could. And not only you, it appears. He was discharged and lost everything because of your case. I wonder how many more like him hold a grudge?"

"It appears we've been rather protected by the threats of MI5 to those in the army who wanted retribution. No doubt this one was freelance if he's been given a dishonourable discharge."

"You do need to be careful, Phelps."

Neil grinned. "Oh I think I know who they all are, Inspector. I'm only sorry I wasn't here when this one came."

"What are you intending?"

"You really don't want to know. In fact, it's probably better if you don't."

"Phelps, I am warning you. Don't go overboard or I can't protect you."

"What makes you think I need protecting." Neil stood up and walked over to the window, then turned and pointed at the bullet holes in the desk. "I don't carry a gun. I am entitled to defend myself against someone aiming a gun at me, aren't I?"

"Don't get too overconfident, Phelps. I don't want to have to pick up the pieces when these two fall apart. Janine is upset enough as it is."

Neil held up his hands in truce.

After lunch they sat and looked over the notes carefully noting everything everyone had said.

"He had no friends; he made friends with the other lodger who got himself killed; he never went out except at weekends; he had no friends in London except the girl Mavis he sometimes met for coffee."

"So, he wasn't a recluse if he was friendly with her. Perhaps there were others."

"If there are, I haven't found them."

"Perhaps they've already had accidents?"

"Why are we still looking at Percy Blenkinsop. I thought he was out of the frame." Janine said.

"Because we have nothing else and besides, I have this feeling." Roger shook his head.

"You think he is involved?" Neil queried.

"In some way, although I can't be sure. You said he loved sailing. If that's where he went every weekend then perhaps that's where he is, at the same place."

"But we don't know where."

"I thought he went to the South of England." Janine cut in.

"That's true. Summers said so and so did the girl, which rather confirms it."

"Did she say anything else?"

"Not really." Roger looked at his notes. "Oh. Yes. This is interesting. I asked if he invited her to go and she said no, it wasn't that kind of friendship and besides, he had been invited and he could hardly drag her along."

"Then he was meeting someone."

"Someone invited him and his pleasure is sailing. What does that intimate?"

"That someone with a boat invited him." Janine surmised.

"Dinghy sailing or something larger do you think?" Neil said thoughtfully.

"He would need a passport if they went away from England." Roger said thoughtfully. "Blast! We never realised. That neighbour on Stoat Lane said he waited for the Postman and he had an official envelope. We thought it might be to do with work, but what if it was a passport like the postman thought!"

"Then he could be anywhere and we don't stand a hope in hell of finding him. If he did join a boat on the south coast then it could have been anywhere from Dover to Penzance." Neil was angry now and Roger needed to calm him down if they were to make any progress. Just at the moment he felt as angry as him.

"We need to be ahead of the game. If Percy arrives back on Monday then everything gets out of our hands. If he does not, then others, like MI5 will know what we have been searching for."

"Would any of them admit to the possibility of a fourth key." Neil was seriously wound up.

"I doubt it. That leaves us as the only ones searching and we could be seriously hampered by the security services who would instantly blame Blenkinsop and block any avenue of enquiry for us."

"We need a better plan." Janine suggested.

"True." Roger looked up at the wall. "Our investigation board is out of date but even so it could be useful to keep it, we just need a bigger board."

"Where do we get one of those. They don't exactly sell them at the supermarket." Neil said sarcastically.

"I know exactly what we want. Switch the phone through to the house, Janine, and we lock up here for the day. Oh, and bring that pack of coloured chalks." A change of scene might help to break the tension and lower the level of emotion.

They trooped into their living accommodation and Roger led them to the dining room.

"Janine and I were discussing the need to redecorate this place. The wallpaper is decidedly past it's best. So!" he swung his arm out to indicate the wall "Behold our new board."

Janine giggled and Neil plonked himself down in a chair and put his feet up on the table. "OK then. How do we plan this!"

"Shall I make a new pot of coffee? Then we won't be interrupted."

"Excellent thought." Roger also sat down and sorted out the chalks. He picked out the blue ones for writing and red for highlights."

Janine returned with a tray with mugs, milk, sugar and a clean jug and coffee filter for the machine. Everyone waited until it started to make appropriate noises and the smell of fresh coffee scented the air.

"Right, what do we need to know most?" Roger hovered with the blue chalk.

"Who has the fourth key?" Janine suggested.

"Who, when, where, what and why, come to mind." Neil put in.

"Well mostly we know the who, we know when it happened and where and what happened so that leaves us with why." He wrote a large WHY as far up the wall as he could reach.

"Why did Blenkinsop do it, if he did?"

Roger wrote a list down the left hand side

KEY 1 – PB,

KEY 2 – Summers,

KEY 3 – Sir AMOS,

KEY 4 – UNKNOWN.

"So, PB why would he do it?"

"Money, I would think, he doesn't seem to have any political affiliations that we know of. He never went to a meeting or discussed anything with friends."

"Good thinking." Roger wrote 'Money, not politics' beside his name. "The thing is, why now, why not before. Sir Amos has had loads of files out and none of those have gone missing."

"Perhaps he thought his holiday would cover him."

"That seems very unlikely." Janine put in.

"What opportunity did he really have? Summers was with him and he gave the keys straight to him to lock away. Unless Summers was not watching and he was very daring, when could he have taken the papers?" At the far right of the wall he wrote OPPORTUNITY and under it, level with Key 1 he wrote LOW.

"So what about Summers?" Neil suggested. "From the way he spoke, if he were blamed he would lose everything including his pension. He seemed genuinely worried."

"He could be covering for not having seen Percy check the file."

"But he never blamed Percy, it was his boss."

"And he went along with it."

Roger wrote by KEY 2 – Summers. 'Stands to lose everything. Very worried. Blamed PB because he was told to.' He took the red chalk and wrote SCAPEGOAT to the right hand side of Blenkinsop's line, then drew a red line from KEY2 line to the scapegoat word. "But he did have a key. Which means he had opportunity." Under opportunity he wrote HIGH.

KEY 3 – SIR AMOS. "What do we know about him?"

"He found the letters missing on Monday morning." Janine suggested.

"But why would he take them? He had access to any papers he wanted and he automatically blamed Blenkinsop."

"Too quickly, do you think?" Neil queried.

"Possibly." Roger mused. He wrote 'No reason or unknown unless political. PB away makes him a natural scapegoat." He took the red chalk and drew a line from the end of Key 3 line up to the word scapegoat. Then under OPPORTUNITY he wrote HIGH.

Now there was KEY 4 – UNKNOWN. "Well that's just it. We know nothing of who it could be so we don't know a motive. But if he had a key why wait until now. Sir Amos has had so many files out. Could he be a trouble maker? Perhaps he took the opportunity of PB being away." He put a red line from Key 4 line to scapegoat. And under opportunity he wrote MED – HIGH, needed to be in the building.

"Why in the building?" Janine asked.

"Because they monitor who comes and goes and anyone unknown would be noted. Plus, it would have had to be when few people were there between Friday evening and Monday morning and security would have noted him."

Janine poured coffee while they stared at the board.

Neil frowned. "Was it timed to coincide with Blenkinsop going on holiday, or is that just a coincidence."

"It's a good thought, Neil. Of course, it is possible there is more than one person involved."

"It's so frustrating." Neil banged his hand on the table.

"Mind the coffee!" Janine exclaimed grabbing the pot to steady it.

"What about the girl. She said he checked the file before he signed for it, but did he. We only have her word for it. Dare I go back to speak to Mavis again."

"So are we ruling out Percy B." Janine asked.

Roger hesitated. "It seems too pat. Everything happening at just that time."

"Like all your red lines show, whoever it was, Percy B was a scapegoat." Neil said. "But where do we go from here?"

"Maybe we need to wait for Monday and see what happens." Roger sighed.

"Something will turn up. You'll think of something, Roger." Janine leaned forward and put her hand on Roger's arm, something she had never done before.

"What do we want for dinner?" Neil asked.

"Oh, is it your turn?"

"If you like. The fridge is fairly full. Sausages, fried eggs or omelettes, beans, fried potato slices."

"I like your fried potato slices. Can you fry some bread to go with it?" Roger grinned.

They sat eating with a bottle of Bulmers cider which was now almost empty and stared at the wall.

"It's like something biblical. 'THE WRITING ON THE WALL'." Neil joked.

"Well unless we think of something we could be doing, it looks like we have time on our hands until Monday. Where do you suggest we go, to the beach?" Roger looked surreptitiously at Janine.

"Well you two can if you want." Janine muttered.

"Come with us Janine, or I'm not going."

"Why not?"

"Because."

"Because it has too many memories you want to forget?" Neil suggested.

"Probably."

"Then we stay here and stare at the wall." Neil joked.

The telephone rang and made them all jump. The house phone was in the hall and Neil went to answer it. He returned and looked at Roger.

"There's an Inspector Harwood wants to speak to you."

CHAPTER SIX

oger came back into the dining room and looked quite shocked.

"They've found the man. The one who pushed Billy Norman. He wasn't a drunk, just homeless. He had something on him that led them to a homeless hostel where he had been staying. When he left he was in high spirits, said he had been offered a job with living accommodation. If some kids hadn't been on private land he would never have been found for weeks or even months."

"How did he die?"

"They're not sure yet, but it looks like it wasn't natural."

They all sat silently taking stock of their thoughts.

"We're back to Percy Blenkinsop." Neil said.

"It looks like it. But at least we now have a possible direction. He was found off the Reading road a few miles past Ascot."

"Why do we need to find where he went sailing?" Janine asked.

"Friends, Janine. He must have made friends there to be invited to go sailing with them. What we need now is to find where in that direction you can go sailing, preferably not on a river. If he goes every weekend it must be a club."

"He could just be going to a houseboat somewhere."

"Thank you, Neil!"

"Well he could. Although who would invite him sailing if he just sat in a houseboat."

"Where can we find out about sailing clubs? Is there a central register?"

"I doubt it. Start by phoning Bracknell then Reading town hall and ask them who would know, possibly they have a leisure department. If not, pick large towns in that direction and try them. We just have to keep trying until we get a break through. I have arranged to speak to Harwood tomorrow to see what I can find out."

"Be careful, Roger. MI5 warned us off."

"If I go tomorrow I can be out of London before they know anything is happening."

"Are you sure MI5 believed us?"

Roger chewed it over in his head. "I wonder. They know us, so perhaps they realise we have more information. Why would they let us go so easily?"

"If they have." Neil frowned. "Do you trust them?"

"No. We need to be very aware of everything that happens if we have any hope of succeeding."

"Can we go and see about that entry intercom?" Janine asked, hopefully.

"Yes. Even with Neil here with you it needs doing quickly."

"I gather I am not going to London with you." Neil sounded a little put out.

"Who is going to protect Janine. Also, you don't know Inspector Harwood."

"I suppose you want to take my car?" Neil groaned.

"Good grief no! If it got so much as a scratch I would never hear the end of it. Besides, you need it to take Janine shopping and you both need to stay together when out of the house. I'll hire a rental car for a week."

"I imagine MI5 know the car registration anyway." Neil suggested.

"Then a rental car would be more anonymous. Bit late to phone tonight, but I'll pack a bag in readiness." Roger stood up and stretched. "I'm for bed. I'll wish you both goodnight. We'll continue making plans in the morning."

Friday morning they congregated in the office. Roger's bag sat on the floor and Janine had already telephoned the Police to ask for the name of the firm which fitted entrance door security. They had an appointment at eleven.

"What's the matter, Janine?" Roger leaned forward to touch her arm as she sat staring through the net curtains with a definite frown on her face.

"A man has just walked past."

"Is that strange?"

"Not particularly but I saw him walk the other way a few minutes ago. Where could he have been to? I saw him earlier too."

Neil looked at Roger and pulled a face. "I don't like this."

"Nor do I. It looks as if we could be under surveillance. We need to check when we go out."

The telephone made a 'ting' but never rang. Roger picked it up to listen.

"The line could be being tapped."

"To have a tap put on at the exchange would make it someone official. We could ask Inspector Dutton to check. If he is allowed to, that is. It does mean that everything we do by phone will be monitored."

"I think that answers your thoughts on whether MI5 had actually believed us."

"How can you keep in touch!" Janine worried.

"We'll have to do what we did before we had the telephone. I phone at a set time to the pub phone. I could give you three rings, say one hour before to give you time to go out."

"Do it twice, the first might not be you."

"OK, let it ring three times and do it twice. Then I phone the pub. I could give you a number to contact me so take something to write on."

They piled into the car to visit the security company and Neil pulled out of the driveway.

"Don't look too obviously. Is there anyone around on your side, Janine?"

"No, the road's clear on my side."

"There's a car with what looks like two men in it just down the road my side. Don't drive too quickly, Neil."

By the time Neil had turned the corner and driven slowly down the road the car had come round the corner. When they arrived at the Police Station Neil stayed in the car with Janine while Roger went in and requested a worried Inspector to check if there was a tap on their phone. Dutton was evasive, so Roger thanked him for the information.

"I never said anything." Inspector Dutton insisted.

"You didn't need to." Roger informed him.

The salesman started his usual spiel when Janine interrupted him.

"We are here to see about security for our front door. I don't feel safe."

"Of course. Miss. We have the usual safety chain, or course."

"We had one. We need a proper secure system. You were recommended by the Police."

"Perhaps if you could come and see our demonstrations."

"So this is the intercom." Neil inspected it. "How can you tell who is there, you can't see them?"

"They speak to you, sir." The salesman was perplexed. He was not used to dealing with young people and had presumed it was for a flat or house.

Roger saw his bemusement. "If I could tell you what we require, and perhaps why, then you might understand. We are Williams, Mathers and Phelps, Private investigators. A few days ago, when Miss Mathers was alone, someone broke the security chain to gain access and tried to shoot her. We need serious protection, sir. Some way of knowing who is outside without having to open the door."

"Shoot her!" He turned in shock to Janine. "Are all right, Miss? Did they catch him."

"Yes, they did, and I am quite well, thank you, but I need to know who is in the porch and who to allow entrance."

"Well this is a camera to show who is there."

"Can you see in the dark?"

"Well no, you need a light."

"If she switches on the light he will know she is there."

"Ah, well perhaps a light which is movement activated?"

"Yes. Roger, can you look down at the speaker so I can see you on the camera. Now can you tell who that is? I need to see his face."

"There is the simple door viewer. Through this you can see who is outside."

"With the light you can see even on a dark night, and with the intercom you can talk to them." Roger turned to the bewildered salesman. "Camera, viewer, motion light, intercom and security chain. How soon can you fit them?"

"Perhaps you would come to the desk and we can arrange it." Said the overwhelmed salesman.

The three sat in the car and laughed. "What a bigot of a salesman, I can't stand people you look down on you because you're young."

"Or female." added Janine.

"Can you see the car?"

"They're at the end of the road, but I need to phone the car rental company and I am loath to do it from home."

"OK. Well the pub should be open by now."

They left the car in the pub yard and sat drinking a soft drink while Roger made arrangements to pick up the car that afternoon and took a note of the phone number of the pub's payphone.

"We are definitely being followed." Neil looked in his rear view mirror. "If I didn't know I might not realise, but since we do know then they're easy to spot."

"We are going to have fun losing them this afternoon.

* * *

Roger lay on the back seat of the car with his bag on the floor. Janine sat in the front with Neil driving.

They started by driving to the railway station and parking near the door. The car had only one person this afternoon. No doubt the other had been forced to stay to watch for Roger leaving the house. The driver parked a little way across the car park.

Janine entered the station with her bag on her shoulder and the driver hurried after her. Several minutes later she reappeared with a train timetable and passed the car driver. Neil sped away from the station leaving the following driver to sprint to his car in the hope of following them. A few turns and they were sure they were no longer being followed, as Neil pulled up outside the car rental firm. Roger rolled out and dragged his bag after him.

Janine opened her door and put her hand on Roger's arm. "You will take care, won't you?"

Roger smiled. "Of course I will. And Neil, take care of Janine."

"Don't I count!" Neil grumbled.

Roger laughed again. Janine was definitely softening in her aversion to being touched. Perhaps the gypsy fortune-teller at Battersea was right. He glowed in hope as he waved them away.

The frustrated driver found them again in the last few hundred yards home. Somewhere in the distance was a lonely figure standing behind a tree. What a pity it wasn't raining!

CHAPTER SEVEN

The first visit Roger made was to Inspector Harwood. Luckily the sergeant on the desk was different and phoned up to the Inspector without comment.

Inspector Harwood was like a different man. He stood to meet Roger and held out his hand.

"Good to see you again, Mr Williams. I gather you want to know more of the details of where he was found?"

"I must admit I am relieved he has been found."

"Why were you so sure he would be dead?" Harwood queried.

"It seemed to be the most plausible outcome." Harwood frowned at him. "Billy Norman was a very quiet man so was the other man at his lodgings. He had no real friends, so when they became friends it was unusual for both of them. The lodger is missing and we have been searching for him. He took Billy with him one weekend, where to, we have no idea, but he must have been introduced to people. Three days later he is dead. Why, Inspector?"

"Smells bad."

"Exactly. It seemed too much of a coincidence and I don't really believe in coincidences. Are you dealing with the case or is it Bracknell. I would like to see exactly where he was found."

"Bracknell are but I am liaising with them. I'll give them a ring and tell them to expect you."

"Thank you for your help. Sorry I balled you out. It is really important to me."

The Inspector grinned. "I called you a few names after you left, but when DS Parry told me who you were, I felt about two inches tall. If there is anything I can do to help don't hesitate to get in touch." He held out his hand and Roger shook it in genuine friendship.

The first call in Bracknell was to find somewhere to stay. At least he was out of London and not liable to be noticed by any of Lionel's men.

He found a pub which had a room to rent, although he doubted many used it, it had that run down feeling. It must be depressing for travelling salesmen to stay in places like this.

Inspector Langton had left for the evening but would be there first thing in the morning. Roger left his request for an interview and asked if he could be shown where the recently found body had been discovered. Then all he could do was find the telephone in the pub and phone home. Three rings, stop, three rings, stop. He looked at his watch, one hour to wait, he may as well go and find some food. He only hoped it was less depressing than the room.

"Do you always work on a Saturday, Inspector?"

"Only for murder. Do you, Mr Williams?"

"Like you, I do what is necessary. I can't actually say I have days off. We make the most of the time between cases."

"Exactly. I understand you want to see where he was found. Is there a particular reason?"

"Someone put him there and I want to get the feel of how they got him there and where the access was. Was he carried or dumped from a car, that kind of thing."

"Are you sure you aren't a policeman, Williams?"

"I did think about joining but our local DI said it could be years before I came off traffic duty and made it into plain clothes, especially at a holiday place like Bournemouth. The other two needed some way forward and Dutton suggested investigations. Actually, I think someone in court made that suggestion but it was probably meant as sarcasm."

Langton laughed. "It's not every private dick we take seriously, you know."

"I don't expect it is. And I am sorry I can't tell you about the case which led me here. Let's just say whoever is involved could live in this direction. I hope so or we are literally up a gum tree."

"I wish you luck. Any information you find out we would like to be told, of course."

"I have no doubt someone will tell you at some stage, although it may be someone more exalted than me. I just do the donkey work."

"Now why don't I believe that" Langton laughed.

The land was off the road and rather marshy although it was on a small rise where the body had been found.

"Not dumped by someone passing, then."

"No. And no tyre tracks that can help us because of the time which elapsed."

"Was the body moved later or put here at the time, do you think?"

"Forensics think it was here since shortly after death and there are no signs of it being moved. We did find it over a week ago, we just had no idea who it was."

"What put you onto him. Harwood said you had something that led you to the homeless hostel."

"We did, but which. They have some clothing donated by a large retail chain which goes to a range of hostels. It took us some time to realise that and it would have taken us quite a time to contact them all. When the memo came through from Harwood he fitted the description."

"And this is private land."

"It is. Even this road which is closest is private, so whoever it was probably knew the body would not be found for some time. The area is rarely visited except in midsummer when the farmer puts sheep on here. The rest of the time it's often waterlogged. It was quite by chance some kids came playing here, possibly as a dare."

"I bet it gave them a fright." Roger mused.

"You bet. Their parents don't know whether to punish them or praise them." Langton laughed.

"Someone knew the area or sussed it out before." Roger said.

Langton studied him. "Possibly."

"Which means a local or someone who passes regularly and did some research. I doubt they live very close."

"You have a copper's mind."

"So I am told. If I murdered anyone, I would make sure the area was suitable and nowhere near where I lived, which would mean research and you would hardly do that in an area where your car was noted as unusual. People notice the most unusual things."

"They do. And they make up stories to fit. Sometimes you need to find the kernel of truth in the centre."

"Can I ask you one more thing, Inspector?"

"Ask away."

"Is there a sailing club or anywhere I could go sailing round here?"

"Where did that come from? Not from the boggy ground, surely."

Roger laughed. "No, a completely different area of investigation."

"Well... Not really. There's the River Kennet this side of Reading and the Thames above Reading. I suppose they sail there. It's not something I've ever needed to know."

"Well it rules out your area then.""

"Good. If it saves me any more paperwork." Langton laughed.

Roger picked up his car and drove around the area looking for other ways anyone could have accessed the area unseen. When he turned off the road into a narrow track a man in the nearby field shouted at him.

"Here, where are you going?"

"Does this go anywhere?" Roger asked.

"No, only to my farm and it's private property!"

"Oh. Sorry."

Well that ruled out another route.

With no ideas left he drove on towards Reading.

He parked in the library car park and went inside. The woman on the desk smiled at him. "Yes, sir."

"Is it possible to go sailing near here? Is there a sailing club of any kind?"

"I can give you what information I have, but I'm not sure if our records are up to date where something like sailing is concerned." She pulled a folder from beneath the desk and opened it. "The only one we have listed is on the gravel pits near Pingewood. Surely there must be something on the Thames as well?" She searched the file. "I can't see anything here. I know there are boats on both the Thames and the Kennet but I don't have any information of a sailing club."

"Perhaps I can start with the one near Pingewood. Do you have any directions?"

She produced a map as if by magic and charged him sixpence. It wasn't a very detailed map, so he wandered round Reading until he found a Smiths bookshop, but their map was not much better. He found a road atlas with easier to follow directions.

Armed with all the information he could glean, he set off south of Reading to find these gravel pits near Pingewood.

Every small road he took led him to another dead end. They all seemed to have been used for the extraction of gravel. He did find a few houses that were all that was left of the village of Pingewood, but nowhere to stay. Eventually he found a pub in Three Mile Cross.

"Do you do rooms?"

"No. How long for?"

"Well a few days possibly. I'm just looking for where the sailing club is?"

"Why?" He seemed rather surly.

"I've never seen sailing on a lake before and someone said there was a club on the gravel pits."

"You on holiday?"

"Got a few days off."

"Well you'll not see much sailing. They only sail at the weekend and it's Sat'day afternoon already."

"I've been driving round for ages. The library said Pingewood, but every road was a dead end."

The bar tender burst out laughing. "If you're looking for Pingewood there's precious little of it left. Miss Townley at the pink cottage up the street, she rents out to someone at weekends, but he's not here at the moment. She would probably be glad of a lodger for a few days." He took an old envelope from behind the bar and drew a map. "That's how you get to the sailing club, but I doubt many will still be on the water. A few sometimes come in for the evening on a Sat'day."

"Thank you. What time do you do food?"

"Hot food, not 'till seven. I can do you a sandwich."

"Please."

"Cheese and tomato do you."

"Yes. Thank you."

Roger sat with his pint and sandwich for some time then set off up the road to Miss Townley's cottage.

It stood out like a sore thumb. Pink. It would have been better if there was some greenery growing over it, like ivy. He knocked tentatively on the door. Her usual weekend lodger was away. Could that be Blenkinsop. Could he be that lucky!

"Miss Townley, the man at The Swan gave me your name as somewhere I might get lodgings for two or three nights."

The woman was a typical spinster wearing a blouse with a Peter Pan collar, a heavy skirt possibly made of wool, and a cardigan which she had probably knitted herself. Judging by the left sleeve she kept her handkerchief pushed up there.

"You're in luck, young man. I have two rooms to spare at the moment."

Roger was shown up to a pleasant room with a good sized bed for one, but which was probably often let out as a double. The sun was shining in, which made the room seem lighter than it usually was, with its patterned wallpaper and dark green and red marled eiderdown over a dark green satin bed cover. There was a Lloyd Loom chair in deep red with residual flecks showing there had once been some gold involved. It contained a frilly cushion with flowers that matched nothing in the room. The wooden furniture was old but well-polished, in fact the room smelled of lavender polish.

"Will you be staying long?"

"Two, perhaps three nights, Mrs Townley."

"Breakfast is at eight thirty and I don't allow food in the bedroom."

"That's not a problem, I intend to eat at the Swan. They do have a good menu."

"Let's hope it continues." She said, rather sarcastically, Roger thought.

Dare he ask. Here goes. "The landlord said you normally have a weekend lodger from the sailing club. Would that be a Mr Blenkinsop, by any chance?"

Miss Townley looked up at him in surprise. "Do you know Mr Blenkinsop?"

"Not very well, I must admit. He is a very quiet man and not given to talking about himself."

"Oh, he is indeed. Been coming here for several years now and I still don't know anything about him."

"He never talks about himself at work."

"Oh, do you work with him?"

"Well not exactly 'with him', but he did say that he came sailing at Pingewood. He only mentioned it the once, but as I had time on my hands and nowhere to go, I thought it might be interesting, while he was on holiday, to see where he went every weekend. I wondered if he was as quiet here as he is at work? I wouldn't intrude if he were here." He hoped he sounded sufficiently reticent.

"He is a very private man isn't he. He's never told me anything about himself in all the time he's been here. I was surprised when he brought that other young man with him."

"Other young man?" Roger could hardly admit to knowing Billy Norman as well."

"Yes, a Mr Norman. He seemed almost as quiet at Mr Blenkinsop but not as polished, if you understand me."

"Oh I do, Miss Townley. Mr Blenkinsop seems capable of mixing with anyone."

Miss Townley nodded as if she knew a secret. It would be his intention now to find exactly what she knew.

As it was still only late afternoon Roger changed out of his suit and took a drive to find the sailing club. Somehow, he had expected it to be a proper building with a large car park. What he found was little more than a wooden hut with large windows, where people could sit when the weather was poor. Cars were parked on the grass verge of the track that led in. At the moment a few people sat at wooden outdoor tables, avidly discussing a problem. The adjoining building was obviously where the boats were stored and repaired. There were a couple of boats still on the water, their sails shining as the late evening sun caught them.

Roger hung back while he took stock.

"Hi." A voice said. "Can I help?"

A man of around forty was approaching from the side of the hut. He was dressed casually and was brown from the sun and wind.

"Oh, I'm sorry, I didn't mean to intrude."

"Are you interested in sailing?"

"Well, to tell the truth I've never seen small boats like these."

The man laughed. "Winston Carter." He said, holding out his hand.

"Roger Williams." Roger took his hand. "I came to see what sailing was like. I never knew there were lakes like this you could sail on."

"So now you know. Actually, there aren't that many at the moment, and this isn't a lake, it's a gravel pit." He drew Roger towards the tables. "Come and meet people."

"Have you found a new recruit, Winni?" One of those at the table called.

"That's up to you to convince him." Winston laughed.

"Peter Finch." The young man said as he rose to offer Roger his hand.

"I'm overwhelmed." Roger laughed. "I only came to see what sailing in a small boat was like."

"Do you want to try?"

"Well, I don't know." Actually, Roger was rather nervous of large areas of dark water and he was feeling glad he was still on dry land."

"You can't come and visit without trying it. However," he indicated Rogers pristine clothing, "you're not exactly dressed for it. Are you here tomorrow?"

"Well, yes. I found a room in Three Mile Cross."

"In the pink house?"

"Yes."

"She'll be grateful for that with Percy away."

Roger tried not to look knowing. "Where is Percy?" He enquired.

"On holiday somewhere. Not that he told anyone where. We're a bit short of real trainers with Sergio away as well."

"I gather Percy tells you nothing. I have come across him in London and I've never met anyone who says so little. Who's Sergio?"

"Sergio is our guru. He's trained many of us and he runs the sailing side of the club. He knows all the influential people who make boats and all the safety rules. With him and Percy away we're a bit short to train you."

"That's OK. Does Percy train as well?"

"Don't you know?"

"I told you. He tells us sod all. He only let slip about this place once. I think if he could have cut his tongue out he would have. We had to pretend we hadn't heard him."

"I always thought it was us. I never realised he was as bad elsewhere. Do you work with him?"

"Not 'with' but our paths cross. Even Percy goes to the canteen occasionally." Roger wanted to go no further with this lie. He was happy to twist the truth a little but making something up could cause a problem.

Roger stayed for a time and talked, watched the boats until they were drawn off the water and stored in the shed. Winston seemed to be in charge of the security of the shed.

"A few of us are going to the Swan for dinner. Do you want to join us?"

"Thanks. I am a bit on my own and in a far land, as you might say."

"The menu looks good." Roger had parked his car outside Miss Townley's to avoid having to move it later, so he arrived on his own. The landlord had decided to speak to him as he entered.

"We're trying to build up a reputation for food so people will continue to come. I don't know what Miss Townley will do if she loses her business."

"Why should she?" Roger was perplexed. Being new in the area he had no idea what the man was taking about.

"The new road."

"What road?"

"The M4. The route will cut us off from Reading. We'll be isolated. At the moment we rely on visitors driving through from Reading. All we can do is hope we can attract villagers or people from Wokingham."

"Won't they put a bridge over?"

"Who knows."

No wonder the landlord was even more morose than most.

Roger made his way into the restaurant area to look for his new friends.

"We thought you'd changed your mind."

"No, I just parked the car up the road. I wasn't sure where you were sitting."

"We often sit in the bar, you can have food there, but since we have a guest, we decided to treat ourselves to the restaurant."

"The landlord was just complaining about the M4."

"Oh that. It's going to be a real nuisance, I know that. Half the club members will be on the wrong side of the road and the extra drive could cause problems especially with the traffic while they're building it."

There were the usual pies, steaks and roast beef but Roger plumped for lasagne. When it arrived, he was interested to know how it was made. It looked like something he could manage at home when it was his turn to cook. Their diet of pies and fish and chips was not doing any of them any good. Even Janine had no idea how to cook a proper meal, and why should she. They shared everything, so perhaps it was up to him to introduce a proper diet.

The conversation was light and interesting but Roger gained no information of where Percy might be or who he might have met. The most he found was that he used to join them at the pub until a couple of months ago when he stopped coming. They had no idea where he went. He had told them he was invited out for dinner but they never knew where. All Roger could hope was that someone tomorrow would be able to tell him more.

Making the evening phone call was difficult. He made the three rings code from the phone box outside the pub when he arrived there, but he almost forgot the time when the food arrived. All he could do was apologise to Janine when he rang twenty minutes late.

Sunday morning Roger was almost late for breakfast. Miss Townley looked a little stern.

"You were late at the Swan." She announced.

"Yes, I went to the sailing club and met some of the members, we had dinner together. I rather lost track of time." He tried to sound contrite. If she was this judgemental then perhaps he could push her to reveal whatever it was she knew.

"I never met the young man Percy brought with him. Was he a pleasant person?"

"Mr Norman? Billy his name was. He was a very nervous young man. He told me he had been brought up in an orphanage and moved from foster family to foster family. He had no-one. I can only hope he and Mr Blenkinsop remain friends, it would do him good to learn from him. I had to give him some help to dress himself correctly when they went out to dinner. I doubt he had ever been invited to somewhere like Mountbeck House before."

"Is that near here?"

Miss Townley looked stricken. "I shouldn't be telling you this."

"I'm not liable to repeat it, Miss Townley. I don't know the area so I know nobody around here. I'm just pleased you were able to help Billy."

Miss Townley was soothed and smiled at the complement.

"Thank you, sir. Are you going sailing today?"

"Well I am going to the sailing club but not until lunch time. I think I'll have a drive around the area before they turn it into a building site for the road."

Miss Townley frowned deeply. "Don't talk to me about that dratted road." She picked up Roger's plate and disappeared into the kitchen. Her body language said everything.

The drive around the area was of no help. There was no sign of a Mountbeck House. He was loath to ask at the Swan so he drove around until he found another pub. A pity it was Sunday or he could have asked at the Post Office. Nobody knew where Mountbeck House was. It might be necessary to start again on Monday morning.

Not willing to ask anyone at the club, Roger was forced to be taken out on the water against his better judgement. He enthused about it as only a man could who never intended to visit there ever again.

With everyone at work the following morning there was no invitation to join them for dinner that night. He hung back to talk to Winston.

"Where does Sergio come from?"

"He's never told us exactly where he comes from. Tom says he's Portuguese but Harry insists he's Spanish. He could be from anywhere."

"Does he live around here or does he come from London like Percy?"

"He works as a general help and security for a house on the Grazeley Road. Not that any of us have ever been there."

Roger took a deep breath. "Is that Mountbeck House?"

"Yes. Do you know it?"

"No, I just heard someone mention the name."

"You'd never know where it was, they just have 243 by the gate, as if it's a normal house."

"Oh, that's why I never noticed it."

Roger drove away as calmly as possible and stopped in a gateway to beat on his steering wheel. "Yes! Yes! Yes!" It was some time before he was calm enough to carry on.

It was only six thirty and he needed to know if Percy Blenkinsop had come home. He knew if he was missing the house would be besieged by midday tomorrow. Better if he went now, it was only about an hour's drive.

CHAPTER EIGHT

Janine and Neil spent Saturday wondering what to do. They took their minders shopping and along the sea front then they sat and stared at the map.

"I wish we had some idea of where he could have gone. The south coast is such a large area."

"What we need to know is what size boat he was on? Then we start looking for where it could be moored."

Janine looked down at the map again. "We could always make a list of what size boats are moored where."

"It's huge task."

"Not if you take it in small areas. We've nothing else to do. Why don't we set off in one direction and make a note of everywhere we find with boats and what size. The weather's good and we can stop whenever we like to eat."

Neil frowned for a moment then laughed. "You make the decisions and I'll do the legwork. OK, tomorrow we have an away-day driving the coast. East or west?"

"East. Towards Portsmouth and Brighton tomorrow, Poole, Swanage and Weymouth on Monday. If it's a big boat that means someone wealthy and wealthy people often go to Brighton."

"I bow to your superior judgement." Neil made a mock bow and Janine batted him with the map book.

On Sunday morning they packed the car with maps, notepads and sandwiches. Although they could afford to eat out on this assignment it still felt like a waste of money.

"Do you think our minders have realised they have lost Roger?" Neil joked.

"We'll soon know when we see how many are in the car when we leave."

As they pulled out of the drive, Neil waved to the watchers in the car, who suddenly sat up in surprise and started the car.

"Are we going to let them see where we go all day?" Janine asked.

"It depends. I think we could have some fun with them. We can confuse them something rotten. After all, they have no idea what we are looking for or if we are just going on a days outing."

Neil drove gently along the seafront at Bournemouth and kept to small roads closest to the sea, following round through Southbourne to Christchurch, continuing along the coast using all the seaside roads. Occasionally they had to retrace their steps when they ran out of road, which gave them the opportunity to check they were still being followed. Janine waved to them as they passed. Everywhere they found an inlet or harbour with boats Janine made a note of the size and type of craft against the place name.

At Milford on Sea they found Hurst Castle on the end of the spit.

"Can we go?" Janine asked.

"It's bit far and we don't have the right footwear."

Janine looked disappointed. "It is a bit. But we can come back some time and go there."

"It looks very old and very military."

"So it should interest you." Janine suggested.

"We'll see."

They drove on further and found there was a ferry from Keyhaven to the castle.

"There you are. We don't need to walk!"

"Not today, Janine!"

"I wasn't suggesting today."

They drove in silence for a while.

"Sorry. I think I'm a bit bored."

"We need to stop for lunch."

"It's too early yet."

"Well for a coffee break then."

"OK. When we find somewhere suitable."

They stopped at Butlers Hard and wondered if they would need a mortgage to buy a coffee. Up through Beaulieu and over the river.

"I hope it's not the Duke who's invited him!"

"I doubt it. He would hardly go sailing at Pingeford gravel pits."

"Pingewood."

"Whatever."

"You are bored."

"It just seems so pointless."

"Don't give up now. Just think how our followers must be feeling. When we find somewhere suitable we'll stop for a proper lunch, not sandwiches."

"You know the way to a man's heart, Janine."

They were over Southampton Water and working their way down the far side, with Janine writing furiously.

"Where was that place again?"

"Netley."

When they arrived at a dead end named Hamble-le-Rice they stopped.

"Do we still have our followers?"

"Yes but I think they're getting as bored as me."

"Good. Let's eat."

They had the usual seaside fare of pie and chips or fish and chips to choose from. They chose fish which was particularly tasty, being fresh from the sea.

"Stay here, Janine. I noticed a petrol station and it might be a good idea to fill up. With luck we may be able to lose our tail when they run short of fuel. I'll pretend I'm going to the loo and sneak off. I won't be long. Keep an eye on them."

Janine ordered another drink and sat staring at the menu and counting flies.

The afternoon was more productive. Around Portsmouth Harbour they found several places of interest which would need some looking in to. One called Vosper Thornycroft and the other Camper Nicholson. Both seemed to make large boats and they could see some in the harbour.

"They look a bit big. Some of them look like naval ships."

"Well the least we can do is ask a few questions, if we need to."

By the time they neared Chichester they drove down to Bosham and parked in the car park.

"End of the line for today?" Neil said, hopefully.

"Definitely." Janine had climbed out of the car and was looking in the window of an interesting gift shop.

"There's a cafe." Neil dragged her away from the window. "The shop will be there when we come out."

There were steps up into the cafe and it was fairly full. Someone was just leaving a table which looked out on the far side and over the water, so Janine made a beeline for it.

Janine leaned back in her chair and breathed a sigh then looked out over the small bay at some houses.

"If this is a dead end how do you get to those houses over there?"

"There must be another road."

"Pity. I'd like to live somewhere like that. Cut off from the rest of the world and surrounded by the sea."

"Looking at the size of the houses I bet they have expensive cars."

"You're car mad."

"No I'm not. I bet they have boats and go sailing as well."

"They're all small boats here. He could be here, just enjoying a holiday with rich friends."

"So why did he say he was not staying in one place."

"Did he! Oh yes, that was what Summers said. He thought he was going walking."

They ordered tea and cake. It arrived in a china tea pot with delicate cups and saucers and a tea strainer. The cake was on a large plate with a doily.

"What a civilised place. I could definitely live here."

The MI5 men caught up with them just as they were leaving the cafe.

They wandered around the building and found where the sea often came up so far some of the nearby houses would be inaccessible. Their road did go around the inlet but it flooded every high tide. They could see a road to the Hoe, as they called it, but it was on higher ground. They wandered to the right and found more inlets and a village green with houses.

"I could live there."

"It's a bit small."

"Not the cottage, that beautiful house." Janine was pointing to an Edwardian looking house which faced onto the green.

"Going to marry a millionaire are you."

There was a sudden silence while what Neil had said sank in.

"Sorry."

"It's all right Neil. It would be nice to be normal and have kids and a nice house."

"Maybe in time you will. Maybe someone will help you to forget."

"It frightens me, Neil. The thought of being alone my whole life. And yet I can't even let anyone touch me."

"It's early days yet, Janine. And you will never be alone. You have me and Roger."

"But what if you get married."

Neil burst out laughing. "Who the hell is going to want me!"

Janine looked at him and smiled. Then copying his words she said "It's early days yet, Neil."

"Let's go home."

"Let's."

* * *

Roger arrived at Stoat Lane and parked in the wider road to avoid being noted by Mrs Garth. There were extra cars parked here on a Sunday evening.

He knocked on the door of number twenty six.

Mrs Bilton opened it then looked surprised. "I thought it was Mr Blenkinsop."

"I'm sorry, Mrs Bilton. Hasn't he returned home yet?"

"No, I'm afraid he hasn't. I expected him last night, or this morning at the latest. He likes to get himself ready for work on Monday morning in plenty of time."

"Unfortunately, I needed to speak to him today. I have appointments tomorrow." Roger apologised.

There was no reason to speak to the neighbour, Percy had not come home and he doubted he ever would. If he was in the mood, he could always come and check if anyone was investigating the following day.

Roger stopped down the road and made the telephone sign for Janine and Neil, then he drove around looking for a pub with food. The only one he found with a sign, informed him they did food every night except Sunday, because they did food midday. He set out for his lodgings, but passed two people eating. He stopped the car in a squeal of breaks.

"Where did you get the food?" He asked a terrified couple. They pointed down the side road where he found an Asian corner shop, from which he bought bread, ham, tomatoes and a large bag of crisps. Not exactly what he had intended. He would have driven back but needed to be near a phone box, so he sat in the side road and ate a very unsatisfactory sandwich.

"He's not back."

"Well did you really expect him to be?" Neil queried.

"No. At least we know we're on the right track. I need to find out more about Mountbeck House, 243 Grazcley Road. I'll go to the Post Office and see the names on the post then I'll go up and see who's there. I doubt anyone will be."

"Please take care, Roger. I have a bad feeling about this."

"So do I, Janine. That's why I need to go there and check. I'll come home tomorrow afternoon. Perhaps we could all go out to dinner."

"You sound hopeful, Roger. We're driving the coast making a note of what size boats are moored where. You may arrive before us." She laughed. "See you tomorrow."

CHAPTER NINE

ools rush in where angels fear to tread, and Roger was no fool. He needed to do a little more research.

The Post Office was the obvious place, and he hoped the Postman was chatty with the staff. He had no idea when the post was delivered.

A pleasantly plump woman was behind the counter.

"I wonder if you could help me?" Roger began. "I am trying to leave a message for Sergio, the trainer from the sailing club. I understand he lives in Mountbeck House. Is the postman due to deliver soon?"

"Oh nobody delivers to Mountbeck House. There's not even a post box."

"How do they get their post, then?" Roger looked surprised.

"Everything goes direct from the sorting office to the company who own the house. I don't know if anyone delivers personal mail, I've never seen anyone visiting."

"Company! The house is owned by a company!"

"So they tell me. If you want to send a letter you need to post it from here and the sorting office in Reading will direct it."

"What a complicated way to contact a friend!" Roger said.

He wandered out of the post office in shock. So, no way to know who actually owned the house or the names of those who invited Percy to dinner. He would need Janine to do her magic on the phone to find the name of the company. Even then it may not tell them much.

Right! Now to beard the lion in his den. Although from what the post office woman had said, the chances of finding anyone at home was very slight.

Roger drove up the long drive until he could see the house. He whistled. Now that was impressive! No wonder it was corporately owned. He pulled up by the front door, got out and walked up the elegant steps. There was a bell pull to one side which he pulled. After five minutes he pulled it again. Still no answer.

Perhaps there were servants round the back. This size of house was not run by one couple, it needed maids, butler, kitchen staff.

Roger walked around to the back. Nothing. Not a car nor a cat. Not a stick of wood for a fire nor a light in the kitchen. Below the kitchen was an underground garage. There was no telling how large it was. He walked down and rapped on the metal door, but there was only a hollow sound and nobody answered. He walked around to the front and got into his car. The woman was right, there was not even a letterbox.

He needed to think. This was worse than he had expected, but more in keeping with the idea that Blenkinsop was involved with dubious people, including this Sergio.

What was it about this house? The drive. The drive looked as if it was hardly used and the width around to the large car park was too narrow for the kind of cars people like this drove.

Roger drove around the side to the underground car park. The garage exit did not point to the side of the house, it faced a wide path between trees. Perhaps there was another entrance. Originally the occupants would have had a carriage, so there must be a coach house somewhere. He drove down until he came to a large storage building. Why would something this size be in the garden of a house like this unless it was either for manufacture or storage. He'd go with the storage. The path led to a large set of security gates just beyond a copse of trees. The ground under the trees was tyre marked with the treads of seriously large or heavy vehicles which had strayed from the paved path.

A slight movement worried Roger, so he turned the car around and drove some way up the back drive keeping close to the edge in order to search for tyre marks. Among the undergrowth there were footprints in the soft earth.

The back of Roger's neck began to prickle, so he put the car into gear and drove quickly away.

What was Blenkinsop involved in, and did he actually know? Sergio did, that was obvious.

Somewhere to think. He drove to the pub but it was not open, so he carried on into the village where he had noticed a tea shop. He hid the car in a side road, although he was not sure why. Call it intuition.

He needed to report back and discuss this with the others. Was this connected to Blenkinsop's disappearance, more than likely. But who had invited him to go sailing, Sergio? He was a caretaker of some sort. But who was his boss and how could they find out?

Miss Townley was waiting at the bus stop so he stopped to speak to her.

"I think I'll go home this afternoon, Miss Townley. Shall I leave the money in the kitchen, or would you prefer me to give it to you now?"

"Well. . ."

Roger took out his wallet and handed a generous amount to her.

"Oh, this is far too much!"

"It has been worth it, Miss Townley. I'll leave the key on the hall table. I wish you well in the future." He never gave her his card. He was not sure he wanted anyone to be able to track him down when they realised Percy Blenkinsop had disappeared.

The door to the kitchen was open, Miss Townley never left it open. There was just a tiny amount of mud on the bottom tread of the stair carpet. It could have come from his shoes, except it was there when he opened the door. Did he abandon his clothes and just drive away? No, this could give him some information so long as he was careful. At the top of the stairs he entered the toilet. If he was in trouble the last thing he wanted to do was disgrace himself.

As he opened the door to his room a hand gripped his arm and dragged him in pinning it behind him. He felt the barrel of a pistol to his head.

"On your knees." It was a strong but rough voice.

"Why, if you intend to shoot me why on my knees. Or is this a gangland killing?" Inside he was quacking. His head was bent forward which gave him a view of two men's shoes. Army boots and polished too. They were serving soldiers.

"So they sent you to kill *me* did they. They didn't manage to kill Janine so you came after me. And here I understood that we were under the protection of MI5." He felt the arm quaver. He dropped to the floor spun the man over and the gun fired into the ceiling. Now he had the man in an arm lock. "Miss Townley is not going to be happy about bullets in her ceiling. Who are you? And why are you threatening me?"

"We rather thought you would tell us?" The voice was much more cultured and belonged to a third man who had entered the room. All three of them wore balaclavas so Roger had no idea who they were.

Roger put his free hand into his pocket and pulled out his official card, holding it out to the officer.

"Private Investigator. Well Roger Williams, what are you investigating at Mountbeck House?"

"There's a man who lives there called Sergio and he teaches sailing at the club. They said he was away on holiday and I wondered when he would be back." Roger tightened his grip on the arm lock. "I don't trust you. Why are you up there when the place is empty?"

"Ah, but is it empty?"

"Yes, I would say everyone has left. The tyre tracks at the bottom gate are not that fresh. Sergio went on holiday possibly three weeks ago."

"How the hell do you know that if you were looking for him?"

"I want to know when and if he intends to return?"

"Why?"

"Because someone who has been invited up to the house has disappeared and we have been employed to investigate."

"Why would he be there?"

"He wouldn't. He went to the south of England, probably to a boat. Seeing as Sergio is a master mariner, according to the sailing club, he could be on his way to anywhere. What was in the large building?"

"Don't you know?"

"No or I wouldn't be asking. Something illegal?"

"You could say that. Who are you working for?"

"Myself. Perhaps you have heard of us. Williams, Mathers and Phelps." He emphasised the Phelps.

"Phelps as in. . ."

"Exactly. One of your ex colleagues came to kill him last week and not finding him he tried to shoot Janine."

"Where is he, did they get him?"

"Oh yes. Janine disabled him and MI5 tied him up. I understand he may walk again, if he's lucky."

"Someone trained you."

"Indeed. We have had a little trouble with you lot."

"How do you know who we are?"

"Very good dark clothing but highly polished army boots."

"Ah. You're astute."

"I need to be with people trying to kill me for no other reason than I upset their plan. Were you on surveillance?"

"For days, you are the only life we've seen."

The officer sat down on the chair and pulled off his balaclava. "At ease, men." The free man took off his balaclava and Roger carefully let go of his captive's arm.

"So you're looking for someone?"

"Yes. Percy Blenkinsop. He comes here every weekend to sail and recently he has been invited up to Mountbeck House."

"What is so strange about that?"

"He has no friends, never discusses anything with anyone. It took us two weeks to even find he went sailing."

"Why is that strange?"

"He made a friend. A young man staying in the same boarding house. He brought him here a month or so ago. He also went up to dinner at Mountbeck House. Three days later he fell under a bus."

"Ah. I suppose it could be a coincidence."

"Hardly. The man who knocked into him went missing. He was found dead off the Reading Road."

The major sat and thought for a moment. "Do you actually know what you are investigating, Mr Williams?"

"Not what I am finding here. I am just looking for a civil servant who is missing and his boss wants him back."

"This is rather out of your league."

"What is my league, Major?"

The two men locked eyes.

"Pity you're not in the army."

"What are you, SAS. I did think about joining the police but I don't fancy several years of traffic duty."

The Major laughed. "Special Operations, actually. We had a tip off but it seems to have been too late."

"Who knows, they may use the whole set up again in the future. You could have a permanent job here!" Roger laughed.

"God I hope not. We're bored out of our skulls"

"I, at least, can pack up and go home. Do you have any objection?"

"No. I suppose not."

"Aren't you going to check up I'm kosher."

"I know you are." The major grinned.

"Perhaps there is something illegal on their boat." Roger pulled out his bag and started to push his clothing into it."

"Do you have any idea where this boat is?"

"Not a clue. Janine and Neil are mapping the south coast ready for if we find some info about the size of the boat. You may be bored with waiting, but we get to be bored with endless useless searches. I take it my hire car is not going to blow up?"

The major shook his head. "You're quite safe."

CHAPTER TEN

"There's nobody there at all?" Neil and Janine had just arrived home and were intrigued about what Roger had found.

"We need you to use your magic on the telephone and find out the name of the company who own the place." Roger looked hopefully at Janine.

"Does nobody know?"

"The sorting office, they redirect the mail. There's not even a post box or letterbox."

"Will they give it to her?" Neil queried.

"Are you doubting Janine?" Roger laughed.

"Is it a large garden with houses at each side?" Janine asked.

"It's almost a small estate. There are other houses on the road, although one side the land is farmland."

"Perhaps one of the neighbours is having a little trouble." She picked up the telephone and rang directory enquiries. "Could you give me the name and address of solicitors in Reading, please." She spent some time writing. "Thank you very much, could I also ask for the telephone number of the postal sorting office." She wrote down a number. "Thank you very much you have been very helpful."

"Why a solicitor?" Neil queried.

"Do you think the sorting office will give me a name and address just like that. The company obviously want to keep their identity private. Roger, did you say you had a map of Reading. I need to know which of these names is suitable."

She located each of the addresses on the map. "Bath Road. That's the best. It's south of the city and away from the centre. Somewhere a farmer might go from Grazeley Road. I need to think up the name of a solicitor."

"Smith or Jones." Neil suggested.

"Be serious, Neil. Audrey Wilmot of Underwood and sons, Solicitors on Bath Road. That should do."

Roger sat grinning, watching her plan the deception.

"You might need to make a noise at some stage, as if I have an argumentative client with me." She picked up the receiver and dialled the number.

"I'm sorry to trouble you, but I need a little help. I am Audrey Wilmot, a solicitor from Underwood and Sons on Bath Road and I have a client with me who wishes to bring a complaint…No not against you, against the owners of Mountbeck House, 243 Grazeley Road, Three Mile Cross. Unfortunately, there is nobody there at present and I am led to understand it is owned by a company. I wonder if you could give me their name and address." She waved her arm and the boys started an argument.

"Just a moment… Mr Fenwick, please let me deal with this. Taking the law into your own hands will only cause problems." She turned back to the phone.

"I'm sorry. I need to contact the company fairly urgently. If I can speak with their legal man then I am sure the problem can be sorted very easily." There was obviously some discussion going on at the other end.

"I know it is not usual, but I can hardly send a letter threatening to sue 'whomever it may concern'. If not contained this could involve the police, which I am trying to avoid." She waited quietly then started to write.

"Thank you so much. I am sorry to have troubled you."

As she replaced the receiver Neil shook his head.

"You were either a con man or an actress in a former life." Neil joked.

"You do realise that by using this phone MI5 will know who we are researching." Roger worried.

"I can't help that. I can hardly sound like a genuine solicitor if the pips suddenly go and I have to feed in more money."

"If Lionel knows then we need to be ahead of him. We need to go to London tomorrow."

"They're coming to do the door security tomorrow." Janine said.

"Then I'll have to go on my own."

"That's not safe, Roger, not with who may be involved."

"We can't leave Janine on her own, Neil."

"Then Neil can stay and I can go with you to London. What are you going to say, anyway? Once we see what the place is like I could always say I was looking for work as a secretary." Janine suggested.

Roger grinned. "Trust you to come up with the answer. Janine and I go to London, you supervise the door tomorrow, Neil, then you go up to Barnsley to check if his mother has returned. I only hope they have not dealt with her as well." He looked at Janine seriously. "You will need to be very careful. I'm not prepared to put you in any danger."

"Perhaps if MI5 come, we should tell them to find Mrs Blenkinsop and keep her safe."

"If this gets any more complex we will need to tell MI5, if they arrive. We weren't employed to deal with murder."

"How do we know what we were employed for, Roger? Did Summers actually know anything?"

"Possibly not, but somebody did. It all depends on what we find at Fleet Jordon Ltd. We'll need to start early to avoid any traffic. We need to be there in plenty of time, even so we may need to stay overnight. None of us know London well."

"It could be that they just rent the place out. If so, then perhaps they will give us the name of who rents it. If not, then we need to find who the principals of the company are." Janine said.

"It would have needed to be rented for several years by another company because of that storage building. I wonder what would have been stored in the building at the back, do you think?" Roger queried.

"Judging from your description of the tyre tracks, it could have been army vehicles, especially with the Special Operations there. Why were they there? It has to be something to do with the army." Neil was adamant.

"Could it be arms?" Janine wondered.

"Why would they be storing arms there, and if so, were they stolen or illegal?" Roger was thoughtful. "Who would want illegal arms unless it was the IRA."

"Lots of countries. Where was Sergio from?" Neil queried.

"Are we getting side tracked into another case? Are we willing to take on the army as well as MI5? We are trying to find where Blenkinsop went and what happened to the letters." Janine reminded them.

"Why?" Roger said.

"Why what. Why did the letters go missing?" Neil replied.

"Good point. They must have been important." Roger mused.

"Or incriminated someone." Neil suggested.

"That is an angle we haven't looked at. Did they go missing because they could have caused someone embarrassment, and if so who?" Roger said.

"Are the two cases even linked?" Neil queried.

"If so, did Blenkinsop go with Sergio? We are presuming that he did." Roger wondered.

"Don't tell me there's someone else he went with! How complicated can this get." Neil exclaimed.

"We need to weed out everything that is side tracking us." Roger suggested.

"But what if it is all involved. You're forgetting Billy Norman. He was killed just after visiting Mountbeck House and his killer was killed almost immediately. Someone is covering their tracks." Janine suggested.

"Which probably means Blenkinsop is no longer alive." Roger mused.

They sat thoughtfully.

"If not, then why are we trying to find him?" Janine said.

"Are we supposed to find him? Summers was told to find a private eye who could always be silenced, whatever he meant by that." Roger noted.

"Why do we keep coming back to Sir Amos." Neil queried.

"I wonder if he has any connection with Mountbeck House?" Roger said.

"If we go looking into him then we need to be extremely careful." Neil was beginning to be very reticent.

"We need to be careful anyway. We know of two people who have been murdered and one who is missing. It's not quite the same as a lost dog. Even our own case was not deliberate murder in the beginning, and it was a cold case by then. This is very much alive and seems to involve Special Forces." Roger said, thoughtfully.

"What is Percy involved in? We don't know. There are some letters missing and he has been accused. Do we say we don't believe he took them? If so, we would need to prove who did." Janine suggested.

"What were the letters that were missing? Could they have something to do with arms." Neil queried.

"Yes, but why would Sir Amos be worried about that?" Janine asked.

"That's true, he seems very worried. He wanted Blenkinsop found and the private investigator eliminated." Neil said.

"Silenced, but I've never liked the sound of that." Roger mused.

"Neither have I. A good job MI5 are tailing us." Neil decided.

"Let's look at this from another angle. Where might arms be going which could involve Blenkinsop and why was he involved?" Roger wondered.

"We're back to asking, was he involved? Just because he went to dinner at Mountbeck House why would they tell him about what was stored there." Neil said.

"We always said he was a patsy. What if he was there for another reason!" Roger suggested.

"Such As?"

"If I knew that we would have solved the case!"

They sat deep in thought for a while.

"If they rent it out how would the people receive their mail?" Roger frowned. "And who built that storage shed. That has been used recently."

"I'll need to contact the library tomorrow to find where companies are registered." Janine said.

"You're going to London tomorrow, remember." Neil remined her.

"Well, we'll play it by ear."

"They have libraries in London, you know." Roger joked and received a sharp stare.

They set out early and were in the west of London by ten o'clock, although it took them until nearly twelve to find Plumstead High Street.

"The odd numbers are on this side, don't drive too quickly."

"We should be able to see the name of the company."

"Two twenty-three, two twenty-five…" Janine counted. "We're almost there."

"I'll park in the road over there." Roger suggested. "Rippolson Road."

They climbed out of the car and looked across the road while standing on the corner.

"Perhaps it's that house over there."

"That's two thirty-seven. That makes that shop two thirty-five and that one two thirty-three. It's an estate agent!"

"Perhaps they do rent out the house."

"It doesn't feel right, Janie."

Janine looked up at him. "What do we do?"

"It could be a cover. Let's watch for a few minutes."

They sat back in the car and Roger watched through the rear-view mirror while Janine used the mirror from her handbag. Nobody went in but a girl came out and walked down the road with her handbag on her shoulder. She crossed a road and went into a café.

"She looks like a secretary, I'll see if I can talk to her."

"I wonder if Mr Abrams of Abrams estate agent is in?" Roger mused. "I think I'll beard the lion in his den.

Janine made her way to the café and went in. She purchased a cup of tea and a teacake, paid her money and looked around innocently for somewhere to sit. The café was not full, but the girl was at a table on her own.

"Do you mind if I join you. You work at the estate agents, don't you?"

"Yes, but I'm only a secretary."

"The very person I need. I'm a bit confused. I'm a secretary to a solicitor and I was typing something for a company called Fleet Jordan Limited at the address of the estate agent. I was in the area so I was interested to know what kind of a company it is. Imagine my surprise when I found it to be Abrams Estate Agency. Do you get post for this Fleet Jordon company?"

"I'm not supposed to know, but we do have post for them, Mr Abrams takes it away quickly."

"Is there another company, say upstairs?"

"Oh no. Mr Abrams lives upstairs on his own, well his parents visit sometimes but they spend most of the summer on their boat."

Janine took a deep breath.

"A boat? Some people have all the luck. I bet Mr Abrams goes every weekend, I know I would."

"He goes sometimes, but not that often. Besides, they go abroad a lot."

"It must be a big boat then."

"I think it is. I heard Mr Abrams mention a permanent berth in Eagle, or buzzard, well it sounded like some kind of bird. I've no idea where that is."

"Do you come here every day?"

"Most days. It gets me out, or they expect me to answer the phone all the time."

Janine finished her drink and said goodbye. At least they were at the right address. She crossed the road to avoid going near the estate agents and went to lean on the car. Roger was already there.

"How did you get on?"

"They have the post but she isn't supposed to know about it."

"That's interesting. Abrams denied any knowledge of them. Stay in the car, I just have to go back and fetch something." Roger crossed back over to Abrams and returned a few minutes later.

"I left my paper carrier bag by his desk."

"Why were you carrying a paper bag?"

Roger grinned and pulled out a tape recorder.

"Let's see if we have anything?"

"Roger! Is that legal?"

"We'll worry about whether it's legal if we get anything."

For a while the tape just picked up the sound of Roger leaving and Abrams saying goodbye, then the office door being closed. Shortly after there was the sound of telephone dialling.

"Uncle, it's me."

"I know but this is important. Someone has just been in asking about the company."

"Of course I said nothing. I denied having even heard of them. What do I do now?"

"They're still in the med."

"OK. I'll be careful."

The tape continued with silence until the sound of Roger's voice apologising for having left his bag."

Roger and Janine looked at each other.

"Now wasn't that interesting. I wonder who 'Uncle' is and whether he is a real uncle."

"If we can find his date of birth we can always go to Somerset House."

"OK Miss Brains. How do we find out his date of birth?"

"Well according to the secretary, he lives upstairs, so he should be registered to vote there. When we registered, we had to give our date of birth."

They stood outside the Woolwich Town Hall where Greenwich Borough Council had their offices.

"Why don't you want to go in?"

"I'm too recognisable." Janine insisted.

"What do you mean?"

"Well that girl, she couldn't take her eyes off the bruise on my face."

"That won't matter here. It only makes you unrecognisable once the bruise goes down."

"I suppose so." She admitted reluctantly.

"You say you are looking for a girl? Why would she be at that address?"

"We're not sure who lives there, whether it is the father or the son. Of course, she may have moved on, it depends on who lives there and what their relationship was."

"And what would you need from us?"

"Which Mr Abrams lives there, which we could take from his date of birth."

"Oh, I see your thinking. Ephraim Abrams, date of birth twenty fifth of September nineteen thirty-seven. Does that help."

"That is definitely the son. Now we can start following that up. Thank you so much."

"That wasn't too hard, was it?" Roger joked.

"He kept staring at my face." Janine insisted.

"Good. That means he won't remember either of us once the bruise has gone. All we need to do now is get rid of it." He grinned.

They found a bed and breakfast in Greenwich and booked in, leaving their suitcases there.

"Where are we going?"

"You'll see."

When he parked the car, Janine was confused.

"It's a fun fair."

"Battersea Fun Fair. Don't we deserve a little treat. Come and ride on the Carousel."

It was good to hear Janine laugh, she did it so seldom and besides, he had an ulterior motive.

After trying all the rides they fancied, Roger managed to steer her to the booths with the fortune tellers.

Janine looked worried. "You don't expect me to go in there, do you?"

Roger put money in her hand and led her to one particular booth.

"Try it. You don't have to believe it. At least you can say you know now they make it up."

She eyed him cautiously but was not prepared to argue.

Roger walked around impatiently, watching for her to come out. If this didn't work then he had no idea what to do. He knew what he wanted for his life and the woman had told him his future. If it was not true then he dreaded the emptiness returning.

When Janine emerged she was very quiet.

"Well?"

"Well what?"

"What did she say?"

Janine turned her head away.

"Is it that bad?"

"Not really. She told me I would be happily married and have children."

"Is that bad? Don't you believe her?"

"Leave it, Roger."

He had no option but to walk silently by her side.

They phoned Neil as arranged.

"Why do we need to keep this charade up with the pub. They know what we're doing now."

"They don't know what we're doing, only about Mountbeck House, Fleet Jordon, and that we are in London. We're going to Somerset house tomorrow to find out who Abrams' uncle is, if he is a real uncle. Take Percy's date of birth with you, if Mrs Blenkinsop has not returned then you could find out her maiden name from births marriages and deaths and if need be, go to Worksop to look for a sister. Depending on where she married, of course. Just take care. Others might have been there before you."

"I will. By the way, I think our followers have given up."

"Until they hear the telephone conversation." Roger laughed. "You've got this number, you can phone here if you need to. I doubt we'll manage to get home before the day after tomorrow."

They found a local café to have a meal and returned for an early night. Tomorrow would be busy.

As they parted on the stairs Janine, who had been quiet all evening, said "She knew what had happened to me."

"Who did?" Roger asked innocently.

"That woman at the fun fair. She knew. Who could have told her?"

"Perhaps she is exactly what she says, Janie, clairvoyant. If so, what have you to fear?"

"She told me the…" she stopped and looked at the floor. "Goodnight," and disappeared into her room.

Roger fell onto his bed and hugged the pillow. "Please be true!" He mouthed.

CHAPTER ELEVEN

he following morning, they were ready to leave immediately after an early breakfast.

"I hope you have your walking shoes on." Roger said, looking down at Janine's feet.

"Why?"

"We're going into London by train and it's a large place as you well know."

They took the mainline to Charring Cross Station, then the Bakerloo tube line to Oxford Circus. Janine was unnerved by the rush and bustle of everyone knocking into her, so she kept very close to Roger. As they stepped onto the tube he put his arm around her back to encourage her on, and except for looking up at him, she never complained. One step at a time!

"Where is Somerset house?"

"On the Strand."

"So why have we come to Oxford Street?"

"You'll see." He was smiling to himself. He hoped she would be pleased.

In places the street was busy with people rushing, so Roger gently took Janine's hand to prevent them from being parted.

"On the way back we'll stop in one of the cafés and have a drink." Roger said to encourage her.

They reached Marshall and Snelgrove and Roger steered her in.

"Why are we here?"

"To get you some makeup that will cover your bruise and make you feel confident."

"Oh."

Janine would have just walked around and chosen something, but Roger steered her into the cosmetics department and to a competent looking sales girl. He did the talking.

"As you can see, my friend has been in an accident and is embarrassed by the bruise on her face. What can you suggest?"

They fetched a demonstrator, who offered to do her makeup for her and suggest what she needed. Roger left her in capable hands and wandered around the store. If he could persuade her to buy the odd suit it would make her look more like the professional lady that she was.

"Oh sweetheart you look stunning!" Roger suddenly realised what he had said and tried to cover his embarrassment. The sales lady looked amused. Janine had no idea how to reply.

"They have a restaurant here." He blurted out.

"Do they."

"I'll just pay for your makeup, then."

They gave her a special bag to keep it in as a present and he thanked everyone for their help.

"I'm sorry. It just slipped out."

"It's OK."

"Are you sure?"

Janine just turned and smiled at him. "Is it lunch time?"

"Not yet, but it will be once you are dressed more like a professional lady." He steered her to the ladies clothing and the display of elegant suits and silk blouses.

"It makes me feel very grown up."

"So it should. You're not a girl anymore, Janine, you're a very beautiful young woman and you need to dress accordingly."

"But these are expensive."

"Only by Bournemouth seaside standards. Good clothes last. Choose at least two suits and several blouses. You could have a good dress for going out to dinner in the evening."

"Won't I stand out.?"

"You mean, will every other woman be jealous of you? Yes." He laughed. "Think of it as an advertisement of how professional and successful we are. After all, you are the public face of the company."

Janine was staring bright eyed into the mirror. "It makes me feel different, somehow."

"So make your choice and we can go and eat."

"You're as bad as Neil for wanting food."

"Perhaps all men are." He walked to a rack and picked out a fitted dress. "Is this your size? Try this on."

When they left shortly after, Roger was burdened with several expensive looking bags and Janine was glowing.

They had a light lunch in the restaurant and made their way out into the daylight, back to Oxford Circus and by tube to Embankment, changed to the circle line to Temple from where it was a short walk to Somerset House.

* * *

Neil set off for Barnsley without much enthusiasm. Surely this was only a loose end. They knew where Percy went at the weekends, they knew he was on a boat somewhere, probably abroad, and he doubted his mother would know much more than that.

But things niggled Roger, and as he was usually proved right, he wouldn't argue with him. All the same, he would rather not be going. What could he tell her about her missing son. 'Sorry Mrs Blenkinsop but we think your son is dead!'

He parked outside the small terraced house and looked around at the water meadows on the opposite side of the road. He supposed it was better than having nosy neighbours staring through their net curtains.

There was no answer to his knock. He opened the letterbox and saw the post sitting on the side table, somebody had been in to check. He wondered if it was the woman who accosted him before.

Nobody came out of any of the other houses. No net curtain twitched. If nobody knew where her sister lived then was it worth it to spend time knocking on doors. Roger and Janine were probably enjoying themselves eating out at posh restaurants.

He walked down the row of houses, knocking on doors as he went. Nobody answered. Perhaps it was market day somewhere, or somebody was getting married or had died. The place was deserted.

He drove into Barnsley and asked at the Town Hall where they kept the register of births, marriages and deaths and made his way there.

"I wonder if you can help me. I am looking for the name of this man's parents." He placed a note with Percy's name and date of birth on the counter.

"If you need a birth certificate you will have to pay. It won't be ready until tomorrow."

"I just need the name of his mother and father and if possible when they were married."

"You don't ask much." The girl said. "Why do you need it?"

"I'm trying to find Percy's mother and she is with her sister in Worksop but we don't know her sister's surname."

"She could be married."

"She probably is, but how do we find her if we don't know their maiden name."

"You would need to pay for a search to find when she was married. If you had her date of birth I could find it for you. I suppose you could get that from the voting register if they'll give it to you."

"I knew it sounded too easy."

The girl laughed." Do you know where his mother lives?"

"Yes."

"Then see if you can find out her date of birth from them. We would know if she was born here." She took his paper and wrote 'Dora and William Blenkinsop'. "Not that it's much help to you. You could have found that out from the Town Hall."

The person at the Town Hall he had spoken to before, recognised him.

"Still asking about Percy?"

"Yes. Well, his mother now. I'm looking for her sister in Worksop, so I need her maiden name which means finding out when she was married."

"I can tell you her date of birth if that's any help. That's on the voting register."

"That's a start."

"It depends where she was married. You might need to go to Somerset House to find out more."

"I'll have to make do with that then. Thanks for your help."

He left with the name Dora Blenkinsop born twenty sixth of July nineteen fourteen.

There was little use him going to Worksop, he had no information to search with. He phoned the bed and breakfast where Roger and Janine were staying and left a message with Mrs Blenkinsop's first name and date of birth, suggesting that as they were in London they could look her up at Somerset House like they intended to do for Abrams. He said he was going home and they could phone him there.

It was late afternoon and he had no desire to drive all the way back to Bournemouth that night, so he stayed. By the morning he felt guilty he had nothing to report. He knew Roger wouldn't have left until he found something. He would make one last visit to the house before driving home.

As a precaution, he parked his car where a footpath led through the fields, as if he had gone that way, then crossed the road and made his way to the end of the terrace, and walked down the row, knocking on doors. There was nobody at any of the houses so he returned to sit on a plant pot in the small front garden of the Blenkinsop house. It was paved and filled with pots of flowers, which were obviously being watered by somebody. Most of the plants were directly into soil in concrete containers, some of which formed the front wall. Neil thought back to when he was young. Everyone left a spare key hidden somewhere, you only had to find it. He doubted it would be under the soil, although there was a small amount of earth on the paving by the only plant in a terracotta pot, stood inside another container.

Gently he lifted up the unidentifiable cactus, spilling a few more grains of earth.

"Bingo!"

Placing the plant pot on the floor, he lifted out the key and checked there was nobody around.

The house was only small, with a narrow front hall, a front room rarely used, a back room that served as a dining room and sitting room with two elderly chairs, several dining chairs and a drop leaf table against the wall. The kitchen had a pot sink with a wooden draining board, a small fridge, a cupboard with a pull-down flap, a gas cooker, a clothes dryer up near the ceiling, and a small wooden table. Upstairs there were two bedrooms and a bathroom with an elderly enamel bath that had seen better days. Everywhere had been cleaned to within an inch of its life.

Neil had not thought to bring gloves, so he had wrapped his hand in his clean handkerchief to prevent leaving any fingerprints.

He went back down to the hallway. He had found no papers anywhere except those on the narrow hall table, where the telephone sat alongside a pop-up telephone pad. He wondered if someone had been there before him and removed any letters. He pressed the letter P on the pad and saw the name Percy (Mrs Bilton). He wondered what the dialling code for Worksop was.

He pressed M for Mary.

Taking out his book he noted any numbers he thought might be useful. At least he had a phone number for someone named Mary who would probably be her sister in Worksop.

He looked down at the few letters sitting neatly on the table. It was because the first one was postmarked Worksop that made him pick them up. This was dated less than a week before, when Mrs Blenkinsop, Dora, should have been there. Should he take it with him? Were they seriously thinking of widening their search? How much trouble could he be in if the letter went missing and it was important to the Police, if she never came home?

He shuffled through the small pile of bills. A postcard.

The picture on the front was of a building in Lisbon. When he read the message he had to breathe deeply to control his excitement.

Whatever Roger had found, this would be better. He put the postcard in his pocket and left, replacing the key under the plant pot and checking there was nobody around to have seen him.

Home to Bournemouth.

* * *

Ephraim Abrams was the son of Eli and Miriam Abrams. Eli had one brother who died young, and a sister. Miriam was born Miriam Huber.

"Perhaps it is Miriam who has a brother?" Roger suggested.

"Huber is a strange name." Janine said. "I've never heard it before."

"A lot of Jews changed their names to sound more English."

They found the name of her parents. Sir Elisha Huber and Martha Jacobs.

"It looks like they were born here or he wouldn't have a title."

They were nervous of asking too many questions. It could give away what they were searching into. They had no desire to be noticed.

"There's a book with all the names and details of anyone with a title."

"We need to look up his name in that book."

"Burke's Peerage." Janine informed him.

"That's right. They should have it in the library."

"How many children did they have?"

"Right. Yes. They had a son Amos and a daughter Miriam. Did all families restrict themselves to one of each?" Roger joked.

"Sir Amos Huber. Could that be our Sir Amos?"

"Bloody Hell! Sorry. We need to find that book and check. The name is different but not that different. He could have changed it to sound more English."

They took the underground to embankment, then the northern line to Leicester Square.

"We'll walk from here." Roger said.

They had both been quiet since leaving Somerset House.

In the reading room of the British Library they sat with Burke's Peerage, the section including H.

"Huber. Sir Elisha. Arrived in England from Austria in 1910. Royal dispensation allowing him to keep his title of baron. Married Miriam Jacobs in 1912. Family seat, Langbeck House near Reading."

"When did he die?"

"Nineteen fifty-eight. Succeeded by his son Amos."

"Is there an entry for Sir Amos Huber?" Janine asked.

"No."

"Look up Herbert."

Janine took the book from him and quickly turned over the pages.

"Sir Amos Herbert, born Amos Huber, inherited from his father Sir Elisha in nineteen fifty-eight. Changed his name to Herbert in nineteen thirty-nine. That was at the beginning of the war."

"I don't blame him. Would you have wanted a Jewish name at that time? We need to think about this." Roger said.

Janine wrote down all the relevant information and replaced the library book.

They walked to Covent Garden and sat in the café down the stairs, where they were serenaded by a young woman playing a violin.

Roger ordered them each a coffee and they stared at the violinist.

"Langbeck is Mountbeck, it has to be."

"And Sir Amos is 'uncle'. Which means he knows we know about the company, Roger. But what do the company do?"

"You mean apart from transport something illegal like arms." Roger muttered under his breath.

"If Percy is involved with Sergio and is on the boat, and Sir Amos knows all of this, why did he ask for Summers to arrange a private investigator to find Percy?"

"Someone who could be 'silenced' remember. I don't think anyone expects us to find Percy."

Janine shivered. "This is getting frightening."

"It is certainly getting unsafe. I think we need to get in touch with Lionel. This needs to be reported to someone and I don't think the Prime Minister will want to know, I think MI5 will."

"Can we go home?" Janine whispered.

"Yes. We need to be somewhere we can feel safe."

They made their way back to the bed and breakfast where they found the name and date message from Neil.

"Lionel can take over from now." Roger said. "We aren't being paid to find his mother."

"But…"

"No, Janine. If she returns home, what can she tell us. If she doesn't return home it's not going to be us who investigate. Best if we leave it to the correct authorities."

"We can tell Lionel?"

"Yes, we can. Pack your case and we'll leave. It will be late when we get home, but Neil will probably be there before us."

CHAPTER TWELVE

"There's no light on." Janine noted.

It was dark when they had arrived at the house.

"He'll be in the back. Let's see if the new light works."

Janine went into the porch and the light came on. She pressed the bell and waited for Neil to answer but nothing happened.

"It's a long way from Barnsley, perhaps he isn't home yet." Roger was bringing the cases from the car and put them down to take out his key. "At least we can see the keyhole now." He joked.

There was no sign of Neil.

Roger checked all the windows and doors were secure while Janine made a pot of tea and buttered toast.

"Do you want me to cook?"

"No, this will do fine. I can't say I'm that hungry." Even Roger was unsettled.

"Perhaps Neil stopped on the way for a meal." Janine suggested.

"It's possible. I'll ring the number he gave us."

"Are you worried?"

"Not really, but you are. It will help if we know what time he left."

Roger dialled the number and waited, and waited. Eventually the phone was answered.

"Yes!"

"I'm sorry to disturb you, but could you give me some idea of what time Mr Phelps left?"

"You do realise what time it is!"

"I'm sorry but we are worried."

"He's still here, in bed asleep like any sane person would be."

The phone went dead.

Roger held the handset in mid-air. "Well thank you and goodnight."

"What did he say?"

"Neil is still there. He hasn't left. He probably phoned the B and B in Greenwich after we had gone. I wonder why he stayed?"

"There is a very good restaurant a few doors away. That could be the attraction. You know Neil and his love of good food."

"Possibly, but we can't wait for Neil to come back. We need to get in touch with Lionel."

"How? We don't have a number for MI5."

"No, but they are monitoring our phone."

"Who are you going to phone at this time of night, it's almost half past eleven. You would need to explain why you were phoning."

Suddenly Roger grinned and picked up the receiver. When the phone was answered he said "Lionel we need to speak to you urgently. This is a matter only you can deal with. Please get in touch as soon as possible. Lives could be at risk, including ours."

At the other end of the phone the voice said 'at the third stroke the time will be eleven twenty-four and thirty seconds --- at the third stroke the time will be eleven twenty-four and forty seconds --- at the third stroke…'

"All we can do now is wait and be careful. At least we have enough food not to have to leave the house. Don't worry, Janine. Lionel will sort this out and if push comes to shove, we can go on holiday somewhere safe while he does."

The doorbell rang at nine thirty the next morning. Roger and Janine had slept late after a restless night and were still eating breakfast. The thunder and lightning had woken them both, and outside it was raining hard.

"It can't be Neil this early. It's stair-rodding it out there, whoever it is will be soaked."

Roger went to check, using the new spy hole. He opened the door to their caller.

"Come in Lionel, we were expecting you."

"Were you really. Perhaps you are rather more astute than I realised."

He shook his umbrella and Roger left it to drip in the hall.

"Come into the house. We're only just finishing breakfast."

"That shows more trust than I was expecting."

"Why, I asked you to come?"

"Did you? When?"

"Last night."

"Ah."

Janine stood as he came in.

"Would you like something?"

"That toast looks inviting."

"Help yourself. I'll just get you a plate." She also brought a cup and saucer.

Lionel looked up and stared silently at the wall they had used as a board.

"You didn't stop investigating."

"Of course not. We have been paid to do a job and we intend to do it. Well we did."

"Something has changed?"

"Very much so."

"Perhaps you can fill me in while I eat. I won't interrupt you."

"No pressure, then." Roger looked at Lionel and saw the glint of amusement in his eyes. Silence can be a useful tool when interrogating someone.

"You knew we were investigating Percy Blenkinsop. I remember you assuring us he was on holiday and would return and confound us. Do you know who instructed us?" Roger looked at Lionel who gave a small shake of the head and waved his hand for him to continue.

"Walter Summers came and said he was missing, or at least some letters were missing that Percy had fetched the afternoon before going on holiday. Sir

Amos instantly blamed Percy and sent Summers to employ an investigator who could always be 'silenced'. He obviously didn't like that idea, so he thought of us. He said we investigate silently and never let on until we know everything. I think he is fond of Percy and hoped we would prove him innocent." He swung his hand to indicate the writing on the wall. "You can see how we were thinking. It all depended on who had access, whether they were taken before the weekend or during. That meant the keys were important."

Lionel was assessing what they had written.

"I presume you have visited Mrs Bilton, his landlady. No doubt you had as much joy as we did. We did learn about Billy Norman and what had happened to him, just a few days after spending the weekend with Percy. The first time ever. I found the timing disturbing. Did you speak to any of her neighbours?"

Lionel indicated for him to continue.

"We had some information from an elderly lady opposite who sits behind her net curtain. I'll come to that later if you need to. The file on Blenkinsop gave no information about his private life and his landlady knew nothing. He was a silent man who kept himself very much to himself. Neil had the car so he drove to Barnsley to speak to his mother and find out where he went at the weekends. There was nobody there, but he did find a school friend who remembered Percy's passion for learning to sail."

Janine indicated the empty cup, offering to refill it, and Lionel nodded his agreement.

"I did two things. I went to see if any of his fellow workers knew where he was going and who he was meeting. That was when you were told about me. I eventually found a girl Percy sometimes had lunch with, but she only knew he was going to the south coast, she had no idea where or who he was meeting. But she did think he was meeting someone. Having no friends, the someone he met seemed to be from where he went every weekend. I also went to see the inspector who dealt with Billy Norman's case. There was talk that he had been knocked, or even pushed under the bus. I asked if the drunk had been found. The case had been closed even though it was unsolved. That was when your men came and found me and you dragged me in."

Lionel spoke for the first time.

"I must apologise for that. They believed you would be more inclined to talk if you felt insecure. You immediately attacked. I must say, I was surprised. I suppose I should have realised then that you would not give up on the case."

"You did realise or you wouldn't have put a trace on the phone and stationed a car outside to follow us."

Lionel smiled ruefully. "I must remember not to underestimate you, Mr Williams."

"Thank you." He looked up at the board. "Percy left his keys with Summers, he realised they were locked in a drawer. He was shocked when he told us. We thought we had come to an impasse. I needed a direction as to where Percy went sailing. It came when the inspector phoned to say the man who pushed him had been found dead, off the Reading road. Reading gave me the name of Pingewood Sailing Club where I found Percy was a sailing instructor, together with someone called Sergio who was a caretake of some kind at Mountbeck House."

Lionel sat up, suddenly alert.

"Did you visit?"

"I tried. Mountbeck was where Percy had been going for dinner each Saturday for a couple of months. It was where Billy was taken the weekend before he was pushed under a bus." Roger looked seriously at Lionel. "I will go into any details later if you wish. The House was empty. There is a back entrance near a large storage building. The back exit had tyre tracks from heavy army type vehicles. I was aware there was somebody there and left. Special Operations are on surveillance after a tip off, but they had arrived too late and have seen nobody except me. I would rather not have to take on the army. That is not part of our investigations, or so I thought."

"And Miss Mathers found the name and address of the owners."

"We realised you would know about that."

"I could hardly phone and risk having the pips go. There was no knowing how long the call would take." Janine huffed.

"Miss Mathers, there is a reason that this agency will be a success and it involves all three of you." Janine blushed. "Tell me about London." He noted that Janine shivered and turned away.

"The company, as you now know, are Fleet Jordon Limited of two thirty-three Plumstead High street.

I won't spin this out. It is an estate agents. I possibly broke the law in accidentally leaving behind a bag with a tape recorder. Abrams denied any knowledge of the company, his secretary told Janine he took the letters away quickly when they arrived. He phoned someone he called 'uncle'."

"Do you have the tape? I would be interested in hearing it."

"No doubt. Abrams is the son of Eli Abrams and Miriam Huber, who is the daughter of Sir Elisha Huber and brother of Sir Amos Herbert. Have I said enough."

Lionel stared into space with his hand over his mouth.

"Billy Norman is dead, the man who pushed him had been offered a job with accommodation, he also is dead. I doubt Percy is still alive. Sir Amos told Summers to find a private investigator who could be 'silenced'. I don't like the kind of silencing they do."

"You were wise to try to make contact with me. Remind me to give you a phone number. Can I hear the tape, please."

While Roger went into the office to fetch the tape, Janine cleared the table.

"You will find Mrs Blenkinsop, won't you?" Janine added.

"Is she missing?"

"She is supposed to be at her sister's in Worksop but we can't find where she lives. We might have found her name if we had gone back to Somerset House, but I just wanted to come home."

Roger came in while she was talking.

"Neil phoned with her first name and date of birth, but we haven't got beyond that." He put the tape in front of Lionel, ran it back and pressed the start button.

Lionel listened intently and played it back several times.

"Keep this locked away. Where is Mr Phelps?"

"Neil's still in Barnsley, at least he was last night. We're expecting him home today."

"Is there somewhere you could go for safety?"

"Like on holiday, while you sort this out?"

"It appears you understand the danger. Of course, they may not know who you are. Did you give him your name?"

"No, I said we were from a solicitors in Reading."

"He could recognise your description. Did he see both of you?"

"No, only me. Janine met the secretary in a café. She won't remember her, she spent the whole time looking at the bruise on her face."

"Does she still have it?" He turned to look at Janine as she returned from the kitchen.

"Makeup bought in London to hide it." Roger grinned.

"I can see you have thought of almost everything. It may take them some time to find who you are. I am sure you are due a holiday."

"Summers may need protection. No doubt he will be asked for the name of the private investigator. It is possible Sir Amos already knows."

"That is possible. Leave it with me, Mr Williams."

Lionel stood to leave. "I won't take any more of your time and I have a great deal to organise."

Neil arrived at eight o'clock looking exhausted but jubilant.

He took one look at Janine and Roger's faces and felt deflated.

"What's happened?"

"Sir Amos Herbert, or his sister, own Mountbeck House, Abrams is his nephew. He is in this up to his neck."

"What about Percy?"

"A scapegoat as we thought. Only I don't think he will be in a position to defend himself."

"Are you hungry?" Janine asked him.

"I ate on the way."

"I thought you might. I'll make some coffee." Janine bustled into the kitchen.

"She's frightened, Neil, and I don't blame her. I've told Lionel and they can sort it from here. People are dying because of this."

"We haven't found Percy or where he went." Neil said.

"I doubt we will."

"How about this?" Neil drew the postcard from his pocket.

Roger whistled. "Where did you get this?"

"Everyone up north leaves a key in the front garden."

"Will it be missed?" Roger said.

"I doubt it. Somebody had been in and picked up the mail. There was a letter there from Worksop, dated when Dora should have been there. I left that for anyone official to find."

"You think she has been dealt with?"

"Yes. This was the only paperwork in the whole house."

"Did you leave any finger prints?"

"What do you take me for! I wrapped my handkerchief around my hand. And I've got phone numbers, probably for her sister."

"I'll let Lionel know that. He agrees that we should go on holiday where Sir Amos and his compatriots can't find us."

"But now we know where Percy went." Neil insisted.

"And the name of the boat, but not who was on it." Roger added.

Janine came in with fresh coffee.

"Look at this Janine. It's even got the name of the boat."

"Manderina III. That's not what the girl from Abrams said."

"Did she say the name of the boat?"

"No. I think it was the berth. That's where they moor up isn't it."

"Where was it?"

"Eagle or buzzard. It just sounded like a bird of prey, she said."

"You've been along the coast, is there anywhere like that in your list."

"Not that I can think of." Janine replied.

Neil was almost asleep.

"Leave it until tomorrow then we can make decisions about where to go and what to do. It's been a fairly traumatic day for all of us."

"If we go abroad we'll need passports." Janine began to say.

"Tomorrow, Janine."

CHAPTER THIRTEEN

"W hen do you need to return the car, Roger?"

"Good point. I did tell them I might need it for longer. It should be back today."

"We can take it back this morning, and can we go to the library?"

"The Library?"

"Or a good bookshop. I need a list of birds of prey."

"And here I thought our Janine was looking for relaxation. I might have known it was work." Neil laughed.

"We could go to a travel agent and see what holidays are available at short notice." Roger suggested

"If we found out where the boat went, we could go to the med and check on them."

"Neither of you want to give up on Percy, do you?" Roger surmised.

"If his mother is still alive, what do we tell her. 'Sorry we never bothered to find out'. Besides, if we find him, we get another thousand pounds." Janine was adamant.

"Do you think they'll pay?"

"It's on the agreement Summers signed." She insisted.

Roger grinned. "So it is."

"Where do you fancy going on holiday, Scotland, Cornwall or abroad?" Neil said.

"I thought we were..."

"Looking for Percy." Neil said. "That means going abroad. None of us has a passport."

"We can get a one year one from the Post Office for going to Europe. We'll need our birth certificates."

"You mentioned passports last night, Janine."

"Well I know it takes weeks to get a proper one, one you could use to go to America, but if you're only going to Spain or France I knew you could get one easily. Did you remember we are only allowed to take fifty pounds each with us?"

Roger looked surprised. "Even for a business trip?"

"I think so."

"How can you rent anywhere on that kind of money."

"I think they expect you to book and pay before you go."

"That does restrict us. If we want to follow where Percy and the boat went we need to be able to cross borders."

"Can't we change money abroad?" Neil questioned.

"What difference does that make?"

"How do they know if we have some extra money in our suitcases?"

"Neil! Actually, that's a good point. I don't expect they restricted themselves to fifty pounds each on the boat. How would they pay for fuel?"

"Perhaps they have a foreign account." Janine suggested.

"Enough talking, everyone get their birth certificates and we get moving. We need to get to safety as soon as possible."

"Where is safe?"

"Anywhere away from here, Neil. If Summers has told Sir Amos who he has employed then we are in danger. Lionel understood that."

They delivered the car back to the rental company and drove to the centre. "You go into the travel agent, Neil, and I'll go with Janine to the Library."

Neil was about to complain until Roger said quietly "We don't leave Janine alone." Neil nodded and they parted company.

The woman looked at Neil in a way which gave him little hope.

"Are there any holidays in Europe leaving within the next few days?"

She lowered her eyelids.

"The next few days, why the short notice?"

"Is that any business of yours. We want a holiday abroad, are there any places available?"

"You said 'we', is it just you and your wife?" She looked deliberately at his wedding finger.

"I am not married and there are three of us, two men and one women, we need two rooms."

"The holiday companies disapprove of cohabiting when not married." Neil doubted the tour companies cared a jot if people slept together.

"Who said anyone was cohabiting. Two men and one woman, why should that be a problem." Neil's voice had risen to almost shouting. "One room for the female, one for the two males."

"I see. Two men with one woman." She sniffed. "How degenerate can you get."

Neil was on the verge of climbing over the desk and picking her up by her cardigan.

A man, probably the manager, came out of the back room.

"Are you having trouble, Miss Williamson?" he stared coldly at Neil.

"No, she is not, I am. It appears unless one of us is married we are not allowed to go on holiday together. I doubt you have three rooms available in the next few days, not to mention the extra cost. We don't even want three rooms, Roger and I are prepared to share, but your 'woman' has a warped mind. I look forward to the day she has shut down your travel agency with her warped attitude. I, for one, won't be using you."

He stormed out, leaving the manager to decipher what that had meant. He didn't want to go with a company and stay in a holiday hotel with other English people, what would they do all day, sit in the sun and worry about how to find Percy.

He strode quickly to ease his agitation, and went to join the others in the library.

"We need the wildlife section. Ask at the counter."

"Do you have any books on birds, especially birds of prey?"

"What kind of book are you looking for, habitat, local sightings?"

"Just a list of birds."

"British birds?"

"Probably."

"In the far corner near the local history."

"Thank you."

"You have to be so specific with some people." Roger muttered.

"I suppose she gets asked for all kinds of things."

They found a book with pictures of all the birds which they hoped would be adequate. Janine turned to the birds of prey and began to read.

"Lammergeier, Egyptian vulture, Griffon Vulture, Osprey, White-tailed Eagle. We don't get these in England, do we? Imperial Eagle, Golden Eagle, Honey buzzard, Black Kite, Red Kite, Buzzard. I know we have those but I've never heard of anywhere called buzzard. Marsh Harrier, Hen Harrier, Montagu's Harrier. It says it's a rare summer visitor. Sparrowhawk, Goshawk."

Neil was walking across the floor towards them.

"What about Gosport?" He said.

"Gosport, where all those big boats were!" Janine exclaimed.

"Well done, you two." Roger beamed.

"What do we do now?" Janine asked.

"We go to the Post Office and get a passport, go home, pack our suitcases and go to Gosport to see what we can find." Neil suggested.

"Why do we need a passport if we're staying near Gosport?"

Neil answered with a grin. "Because cruise boats go from Southampton and anyone searching for us will expect us to fly somewhere, so they may check the airports."

"Do we fancy a cruise?" Roger laughed. "If you two are sure you want to keep looking for Percy then I suppose we need to track him to the Mediterranean."

"Where? The Med is huge."

"We're in a library, let's find a map."

They searched for travel and eventually found a map in the reference section together with world atlases.

"We know they were in the Med because Abrams said so on the tape."

"Wherever it is they must have gone around the bottom of Portugal and through the straits of Gibraltar."

"Would they stop in Gibraltar?" Janine asked.

"Probably, to refuel. It is English speaking."

"If they did then we could ask after Percy. If he wasn't there then he left them before. If he was, don't they need to say where they are travelling to?"

"I don't know that you have to, Janie, but surely they might tell someone. If he was with them when they went on, then we might need to rethink. I suppose it depends on how soon they return and if they call in at Gibraltar on the way back. If he never arrived, then we can work our way back towards Portugal and check with the Police. If not then we see if he is still on board when they arrive back."

"No, Roger. He was supposed to be back at work. How could he possibly have gone back on the boat? He must have intended to fly back from somewhere."

"There're not called police." Neil said.

"Surely they are in Gibraltar? Do you mean Spain? What are they called?"

"Guardia, I think."

"What if we don't find any sign of him?"

"Then they dumped him at sea."

Janine shivered. Roger urged them into action.

* * *

"Where have you put your money?" Roger asked.

"All over me and the case. If anyone looks they shouldn't find it all." Janine answered.

"Mainly on me." Neil answered. "I've put some in my backpack but it is more likely to be searched than a suitcase."

"Why do you still use a backpack." Janine enquired.

"Force of habit, I suppose. Easier to carry than a suitcase, once you get used to it."

"It makes you look like a backpacker."

"That's why it's more likely to be searched." Neil replied. "They'll probably think I am not a suitable person to be on a cruise."

"Rubbish. I'm sure everyone isn't rich." Even so, Janine frowned.

"What will we do with the car?"

"I suppose there must be a long stay car park at the boat terminal, just like at an airport."

"Is there?" Janine looked surprised.

"You've never flown anywhere, have you?" Neil laughed.

"Neither of us have. Have you?" Roger said.

"Once, with the army, but we were bussed in to a separate part of the airport, not where the normal passengers were, but we passed the long stay carpark."

"Do you have the photo of Percy, Roger?" Janine asked.

"Yes, of course, and all the details we need. Make sure you keep your passport safe. Are we ready to pack the car?"

They set out fairly early and Southampton was less than an hour's drive. None of them knew Southampton, so finding their way to the port was not that easy. They passed Thomas Cook Travel Agency on the way and stopped.

The lady behind the counter was a great improvement on the one Neil had argued with in Bournemouth.

"Where do you wish to go?" She enquired.

"On a cruise." Janine said simply.

"But where to, America, Madeira, France…"

"Gibraltar." Roger interjected. "What cruises leave in the next few days that go into the Mediterranean via Gibraltar?"

"The next few days! Well that's a bit short notice. Many of the cruises that tour the Mediterranean are booked up, would you not be better flying over. Many of the cruise passengers fly to Europe to join the ship." She looked at their horror-stricken faces."

"We don't actually want to tour the Med, we just want to go there."

The poor woman looked perplexed.

"Someone we know went by boat which called at Lisbon and then went through the straits of Gibraltar."

"I can get you to Gibraltar but no further."

"I thought they were booked up."

"When people fly over to join the ship in France or Italy their cabins are free for the first few days."

"When is the next sailing?"

She spent some time searching various catalogues.

"Here we are, the Wilhelmina is leaving on Monday evening and calls at Gibraltar." She looked up at their confused faces. "If a tour ship intends to visit Gibraltar then they are not allowed to call at Barcelona or any Spanish port. Franco is very strict. The Wilhelmina itinerary does not include visiting Spain. What will you do when you arrive in Gibraltar? Are you staying?"

"I suppose we need a hotel." Roger suggested.

"Most of the hotels are booked through travel companies who contract for the use of the rooms. Of course, the package includes the cost of flying over."

They were gradually sinking into depression while she searched. Then she picked up the phone and spoke to someone.

"There are rooms at the Caleta Palace Hotel that are not contracted. How many would you need?"

"Two rooms, one with twin beds." He saw the surprise on her face. "We may share the room but I'm not prepared to sleep with him." Roger joked, indicating Neil.

"How will you get back?"

"We may go into Spain and spend some time there?"

"You young people are certainly free spirits these days." She laughed. "I would never have dared to go travelling on a whim."

The next phone call was to the shipping company to book two cabins on the Wilhelmina sailing on Monday.

"You know you are only allowed to take fifty pounds each. It is logged against your passport when you change money, however, as you are going to Gibraltar which uses British currency, I presume you won't be changing money."

None of them trusted themselves sufficiently to answer.

She wrote out the tickets and Roger paid. They were vastly relieved to have that part of the journey organised.

"Where do I park the car while I'm away?" Neil asked.

She took a brochure from behind the desk and handed it to him. "If you show them your tickets they will give you transfer to the ship. You do need to be on board by two o'clock."

They thanked her profusely and went back to the car.

"I don't know whether I'm elated or shattered." Neil said.

"I know how you feel. And don't forget we have nowhere to stay for the next two nights."

"A bed and breakfast will do." Janine decreed. The cost so far had astounded her.

They drove down to find the harbour, then followed the map to the car park, after which they crossed the bridge and drove down the Portsmouth road.

"That said Netley. I remember that place." Janine exclaimed. "There's places down there, I'm sure."

They found the Tellmark bed and breakfast which looked comfortable and was not too expensive, they were all aware of how much money they had just parted with. They booked in and arranged for the evening meal at seven thirty. It would be strange for none of them to be doing the cooking. In fact, the next week or two was going to feel very strange.

"So where do we go now?" Neil asked.

"Gosport. Let's go and see where and what, even if we don't find out anything today. We do need to be careful what we say and who we speak to." Roger said.

"Can we stop for lunch somewhere, I'm hungry." Neil grinned.

"You're always hungry!" Janine retorted.

"Stop winding her up, Neil." Roger laughed.

CHAPTER FOURTEEN

"Are you sure this is the right place?" Janine queried.

"This is Gosport. People have to live somewhere."

"It all looks military to me." Neil said.

"This is the entrance to Vosper Thornicroft but we're never going to get in there." Roger noted.

"I'll ask this man."

"Be careful what you say, Neil."

"Excuse me. Do they have berths for boats here?"

The man crossed the road to lean in to the car window.

"Why do you want to know?"

"Someone we know has a big boat down here and we wanted to see if they had left for their holiday yet." Neil adlibbed.

"Not here, this is all naval vessels. You need Camper Nicholson. They make and repair yachts."

"How do we get there?" Roger leaned over to ask. "This place is a rabbit warren and we can't get in or out."

The man laughed. "Go back to the main road, follow it down and turn left and you come to it."

"Thanks." Neil said, putting the car into gear and driving away.

"Step one." Janine said. "We know which boatbuilder it isn't."

"Let's hope the next is better."

At least Camper Nicholson had an office entrance where they could enquire. The side gate was open and a few men were leaving, they had to remember this was Saturday afternoon. They entered the office with trepidation.

Behind the counter was a woman, who looked like a receptionist, and a fairly old man. The woman was just picking up her handbag.

"I'm sorry to disturb you." Roger said. "But I wondered if this was where boats were berthed?"

The woman smiled. "This is more your field, Bernie." She turned to Roger. "I'll leave you in Bernie's hands. He knows everything there is to know about the company and what happens. If you will excuse me."

She left through the outer door, passing close by them.

Bernie heaved himself out of his chair and came closer.

"What do you mean by a berth, young man. We make sailing yachts and cruisers here. We're not a marina."

They all looked troubled.

"Are you wanting to berth a boat?"

"Not really." Roger continued. "A friend of ours was coming down to join a boat and I'm sure he said here."

"That depends on the boat. Do you know what it was called?"

Roger held his breath. Here goes!

"The Mandarina III. I was sure he said they berthed here."

"Well perhaps they do and then again perhaps they don't. We don't have berths, but we do repairs and refits and we have a pier where large cruisers can come in to be refuelled. What do you know about the Mandarina?"

"Abrams owns it, I think, but Sergio is the master mariner, or so he makes out."

"You know Sergio?" Bernie frowned. He looked troubled.

"No, we don't know him, but Percy was invited to sail with them a few weeks ago and he mentioned him. I wondered when they went and if they had come back yet?"

"This Percy. What does he look like?"

Roger pulled the photograph out of his inside pocket and showed him.

Bernie nodded.

"Have you ever seen inside a boatyard before?" he asked.

The all shook their heads.

"Come and have a look."

"Will that be OK."

"Oh yes. I'm in charge for the rest of the day. Most are on their way home."

He locked the front office door and led them through into where a large boat hull was suspended on a cradle.

"I worked here all my working life. It's hard to let go when you retire. They let me help out like a caretaker. There's a night watchman who comes on later. Sometimes boats come in to refuel in the evening or early in the morning before they leave." He stopped to look particularly at Roger. "What do you know about the Abrams?"

"Not a lot, really. Just that Percy had been invited for dinner a few times and they invited him to join them sailing to the Med."

Bernie look very troubled now.

"They're not actually friends of yours."

"No. None of us have met them."

"I know they have friends in the yard. I would never say this to them, but I can't say I've ever taken to the Abrams."

"Would they have loaded the boat here?" Roger was probing.

"You mean food and such."

"Yes." Roger took a deep breath. "And such."

Bernie stared at him for a while, then made a decision.

"A heavily loaded van came in one evening when I was covering until the night watchman came on. Normally they don't have their deliveries in army vehicles. I thought it strange. They must know someone to have supplies delivered here from stores, plus it was late. I take it that is what you want to hear about?"

"Thank you. And anything you know about Percy arriving."

"They normally leave as soon as they're loaded, but they stayed on the jetty for two days. I saw Sergio bring someone in as I was leaving late on the Friday night. You'll need to speak to the night watchman to know if anything else happened. They were gone on the Saturday morning when I came in."

Bernie led them around the buildings and showed them the loading jetty.

"Haven't you heard from Percy?"

"No. That's the problem."

"Don't you know where they were heading?"

"Nobody said. Just into the Med. We are worried about him."

Bernie frowned again. "Come back and speak to the night watchman. He's on until early tomorrow. Goes off at ten on a Sunday. He may have seen him on the Saturday morning. It is possible he never went. George should know that."

He led them back to the office.

"I'll warn George to expect you. Ring the bell, but if he doesn't answer then ring it again. He might be on his rounds."

Roger held out his hand and Bernie shook it. He nodded to him then patted him on the arm.

"You look an intelligent young man, I'm thinking there's more to this than you're prepared to say. But I won't ask."

Until they were on the road again and there was nobody to hear, none of them spoke.

"An army vehicle, and late, when everyone had gone except Bernie." Roger mused. "Was that stores or ammunitions?"

"We need to speak to the night watchman George." Neil said.

"We'll go early in the morning. I hope Bernie is trustworthy and we aren't walking into a trap."

"Do you need me?" Janine asked.

"No, Janie. You stay at the B and B and sleep as long as you like. You can eat breakfast for all of us."

"If we tell them you'll be back later, perhaps they'll leave you some cereals."

Dinner was eaten in an atmosphere of controlled excitement which meant none of them relaxed.

The boys left at six in the morning.

Roger had the feeling that George was waiting for them. Although younger than Bernie, George was obviously a retired sailor.

"What do you want to know?" George was blunt and to the point.

"About the Mandarina III when she was here. Our friend was supposed to come and sail to the Med with them. Was there anything strange happened."

"Not really. I remember your friend, he looked bright eyed when they pulled out. As to the Abrams, nothing out of the ordinary, except they were late going. She was very low in the water, but then she always is when she leaves."

"Bernie said they usually went as soon as they were refuelled and supplied." Roger said.

"Well I did expect them to go on the Friday, with the stores coming in that early in the morning. I suppose your friend must have been held up."

Neil had picked up on what he had said. "The stores came in the early morning?"

"Yes, just before I was due to go off, and she was already refuelled. I didn't know they were taking anyone with them, they don't usually."

They thanked him profusely and edged their way to the door.

"Is there a reason for this?"

"We just wondered if he had gone. We haven't heard from him recently, that's all."

They heard the door being locked and the light disappeared from the window.

"I hope he doesn't say anything to those friends in the company. They could be in touch and warn them." Neil worried.

"If Lionel has started causing waves, no doubt Sir Amos will already have warned them."

"There were two deliveries."

"Yes. Just how much food do four people eat!"

"I hope they left us some breakfast."

"Don't worry, Neil. Janine organised it that we have a proper breakfast when we get back." Roger laughed.

"She's a real brick, isn't she?"

"I would not have used that term myself, but I know what you mean." Roger laughed.

* * *

When the Wilhelmina left port the three were standing at the rail, watching their homeland disappear into the distance.

"What do we do now?" Janine asked.

"Eat?" Neil suggested.

Janine turned to stare at him. Roger just laughed.

"This is where we find out if we are good sailors. If not, eating might be the last thing we want to do." Roger joked.

"Do you really think anything would put Neil off his food?" Janine asked.

"Could be. Do they provide such things as anti-seasickness pills?" Roger mused.

"Most of the other passengers look much older. What do we say if they ask us why we are on a cruise?"

"Good point, Janine. We can hardly say we are private detectives following a clue. If they get off in Gibraltar they may tell someone."

"Can't we just be on holiday." Neil queried.

"It's just that people like us don't normally go on cruises."

"Why not?"

"We could be doing research for something."

"Such as?" Neil asked. "They're going to ask us what we're researching and try to help us. Or avoid us like the plague."

"That would help. I suppose if we just say we want to know what it's like on a cruise and this is the cheapest one available."

"You could be writing another book, Janine."

"We could say that, I suppose."

"And we came with you to make sure you are safe." Roger added.

Janine turned to Roger and smiled which meant more to him than words.

"We can truthfully say we work together. We don't have to say what we do."

"We sort out people's problems."

"Oh, as if we work for the complaints department."

"Just don't mention a company."

"Shall we explore?"

They found a sun deck, an indoor lounge, a swimming pool, two bars, various offices and the restaurant which looked huge, with pristine white tablecloths and immaculately laid out cutlery.

"How many glasses do you need for a bottle of wine?" Neil queried.

"You have a different one for each type of wine with each course." Janine explained patiently.

"What a waste. Think of all the washing up." Neil muttered.

Roger was curling up with laughter.

"I hope they don't expect us to dress in evening dress." Janine worried.

"There out of luck where I'm concerned." Neil said.

"None of us has that type of clothing. We just wear what we have. So long as it's clean and tidy they can't complain. Even if we do get black looks. We're young people, they can't expect us to dress like them. I bet they save their best outfits for when they reach the Med."

One of the amenities on board was a hairdressing salon and beauty parlour. Janine was encouraged to spoil herself. Which rather misfired as she met Mrs Ashbone, who would turn out to be the biggest busybody on the boat.

There was a fine drizzle outside which brought everyone into the lounge.

"Did you enjoy your swim?" Janine asked.

"It was refreshing. It's ages since I swam. You should have come with us." Neil bit his lip as he realised what he had said.

"I don't swim, Neil."

"No. Stupid of me."

"It might have been better if I had come with you."

Roger looked at her in surprise. "Why?"

"I think you're about to find out."

An overweight elderly lady was making her way determinedly towards them. She took a seat at their table without asking permission.

"Janine. How nice to see you again. These must be your travelling companions." She inspected both the young men which made them squirm inside. Roger had a feeling she was going to be a problem.

"How unusual for young people like you to be on a cruise. Janine tells me this is your first. You must ask me if you need any information, I go on at least two cruises every year."

Roger took a deep breath while he thought out what to say. He never got a chance.

"You must join in the card games tonight. I'm sure more than one will be in need of a bridge partner." She enthused.

"I don't play bridge." Janine said.

"I don't play bridge." Roger said.

"Young people don't play bridge." Neil said sarcastically. "We are at work during the day, not at bridge parties."

Mrs Ashbone showed no embarrassment whatsoever.

"I'm sure someone would be happy to teach you."

"No thank you." Came from all three of them.

"Oh. Well perhaps you could play dominoes."

"Why do we have to play something?" Neil enquired.

"What did you expect to do on a cruise?" Queried the old lady.

"Not play games." Roger said quietly but firmly.

"It's almost time for you to change for dinner." She informed Janine gently.

"Why. What is wrong with what we are wearing?" Neil muttered.

"You don't understand cruising at all, young man."

"Not your kind, obviously. We came for a holiday, not to join an old peoples club." He stood up and walked away.

"What an unsociable young man." Mrs Ashbone declared.

Janine stood. "If you will excuse me, Mrs Ashbone, I need to go to my cabin." Roger made a point of accompanying her.

"She could certainly be a problem. I'll keep an eye on her."

"Earlier she kept asking about what we do and why we're here, and why I'm not married. I noticed a book shop earlier. I think I'll buy a book, stick my nose in it and ignore her. Perhaps she will get the message."

"Somehow, I'm not sure she will. Don't worry, Janine, we'll deal with her, even if it means Neil and I standing guard over you."

"She was not impressed with him at all."

"I'm not surprised. Wealthy people like her are hardly likely to have ever met a squaddie like Neil. I doubt she knows they exist, sailing on her two cruises per year. She probably hardly reads an English newspaper, and expects to be protected as of right without caring who does it."

"I'll see you in the lounge before dinner. And no, I am not going to change. I don't have enough dresses. This is the best I have, and that's only thanks to you insisting. I'm keeping the thinner ones for when we get further south."

Janine walked off towards the book shop and while Roger would have loved to follow her, he knew he mustn't push his luck. Softly softly catchee monkey, as the saying goes.

At dinner there was an announcement about the film 'Breakfast at Tiffany's' showing in the theatre that evening. None of them had found the theatre or even realised it existed. Apparently, the cabaret would be joining the boat at Marseilles, so they were restricted to films.

They decided anything was better than watching elderly cruiseites playing card games.

Mrs Ashbone was ploughing her way through a large breakfast when they sat down. The weather had churned up the sea and it had been rough as they passed the Bay of Biscay. They were now in the true Atlantic and there was a stiff breeze blowing.

"I think I will find a sheltered spot on the sun deck and read." Janine announced.

"At least it will keep Mrs Ashbone away from you."

"That was my thinking." Janine laughed. "Am I being a wimp?"

"She asks too many questions and demands answers. You could be compromised into accidentally giving something away."

"It's not that I don't want her to know anything, it's just that we can't afford to compromise our investigation."

When Janine settled herself in the fresh air under a sun shade, Roger and Neil hovered on the periphery, on guard duty.

"Surely she won't come out here? She's just a nosy old woman." Neil said.

"That kind never let go once they get their claws in. What else does she have to do on her two cruises a year."

"Play cards." Neil muttered.

"I wonder how many people have locked themselves in their cabin for the whole cruise to avoid her and her interrogation."

"What do we do if she comes?"

"Cut her off. Divert her away and I'll do the rest. Janine is too fragile to have her holiday spoiled by that woman."

It took Neil a moment to realise what he meant. He knew Janine so well, it had never occurred to him that she might not cope with this situation.

When Mrs Ashbone braved the sun and wind to hone in on Janine, she was cut off by a pincer movement.

"Mrs Ashbone, can I have a word with you." Roger took her arm and led her to the far side of the sun deck and sat with her in the direct sun. "Would you like a drink. How about a cup of tea?" He suggested.

She looked at him rather bemused.

"I was just going to sit with Janine." She began.

Roger nodded to Neil to return to watch over Janine.

"The thing is, Mrs Ashbone, Janine is here to recuperate. A while ago Janine was ...injured." He decided. "Physically she is healed, but it only takes a little to upset her, which happened recently. We decided that, rather than a noisy hotel with children splashing about in a pool, she would recover better sitting quietly with a book, and falling asleep in the fresh air and warmth available on a cruise, where there were not likely to be noisy children. I know you are interested, but in this case, I can assure you that if you knew the whole story, you would wish you hadn't asked. Just let her heal, Mrs Ashbone."

"I didn't realise. She never said."

"She doesn't wish to talk about it, Mrs Ashbone. She would rather forget. Let her rest, please."

Janine noticed her glancing her way, but at least she went back to the lounge and her card playing friends. The book was interesting, but gradually she fell asleep, as Roger had intended. When the sun went around and began to fall on Janine, Roger gently woke her and they went to the bar for a cool drink. Neil was already there.

Roger paid a visit to the bookshop and asked after a particular book which was not in stock. They did order books, but the soonest they could get it would be Marseilles. He gave the order under the name of Mrs Ashbone. If she wanted to know, then he would tell her. When she realised, he thought it might just spoil her cruise.

Late that evening they docked in Lisbon for the night. Some people chose to leave the boat to find the nightlife, but most wandered the decks or sat in the bars, looking out over the harbour.

Thursday morning there was an excursion around Lisbon. When the three saw the group gathered, they were pleased they had decided not to go. They did wander around the port area but never went far. They found a café to try the local food, but decided as they had no Portuguese currency, whatever that was, they preferred the food on board ship which was already paid for. With most of the older, fitter members away on the busses, the boat was quiet and they could indulge themselves in swimming and reading.

At six, the boat weighed anchor and left for the trip to Gibraltar. All three watched the coastline as they leaned on the railings.

"I actually think I like cruising." Janine said, surprising the other two.

"If only there weren't any Mrs Ashbones." Roger whispered, standing close to her to prevent anyone hearing. He let his hand brush hers, and she smiled at him, so he took her fingers in his and hoped she wouldn't complain.

That night they packed. In the morning they would be getting near to Gibraltar, and they needed to see what the terrain was like through the straits. Especially if they needed to travel on land in the opposite direction.

From six o'clock the following morning, they watched as they passed Faro in the distance. Then took it in turns to eat breakfast, with one of them making notes. The announcement mentioned Cadiz in the distance, and the nearby town of Jerez where the sherry came from, then they were able to see the coastline both sides. The announcement said Tangier on their right, and on their left, Tarifa. Then everyone could see Gibraltar standing tall as they drew nearer.

When they fetched the luggage ready to disembark, Roger left a note for Mrs Ashbone, telling her there would be a book waiting for her when she reached Marseilles. 'How Many Murders Does It Take?' by Janine Mathers.

CHAPTER FIFTEEN

"**W**here are they taking us?" Janine murmured quietly.

"We've got camp beds on the beach, I expect." Neil joked.

Where most visitors climbed stairs or went up in a lift, they were being taken downstairs, below street level.

"I suppose there will be windows?" Roger whispered.

Their rooms had balconies which were almost over the sea. Below them was a walkway which was out of sight unless they leaned out. Somewhere down there, they were told, there was a viewing platform. Janine had no wish to view the sea from that close. She closed the windows and shut out the sound of the waves breaking on pebbles.

Roger appeared at her door.

"Will you cope?" He asked with concern.

"I'll keep the sliding windows shut."

"Won't it get too stuffy."

Janine shrugged.

"I gather all the upstairs ones are for travel companies."

"What happens if there's a bad storm. Do you think the spray will come into your room?"

"That would be interesting. Even we would need to close the windows if that happened. They're nice rooms, Janine."

"Yes, they are. I've never had anywhere this posh before with this much room. I could get used to it."

"Make the most of it, who knows how long it will last." He ducked out of the door and went back to unpack.

The afternoon was spent finding their way around the hotel and sitting on the terrace with a drink. In Janine's case, a pot of tea. Roger watched her gradually relax as the warmth wrapped around her and she sank back into her chair.

"If we stay here long I shall need more summer clothing." Janine noted.

"Good idea!" Roger said. "You can wander around the shops while we investigate the marina and see what we can find out. Buy a bathing costume."

"I can't swim." Janine insisted.

"That doesn't stop you paddling in the pool at the shallow end, especially with one of us to hold you." Roger suggested, hopefully.

"There's the steps in, they can't be more than a few inches deep." Neil was not going to be limited by Janine's panic attacks.

Roger had a smile on his face at the thought of Janine lying on a sun lounger in a bathing suit, or holding her in the warm water.

At dinner, they were allocated a table in a corner, obviously all the others were for tour company guests.

"Shall we walk into town."

"It's further than you think. We should get a taxi." Roger suggested.

"It gets dark earlier here."

"The nearer you are to the equator the shorter the days, but they don't have the dark winter evenings we do up north."

"I remember that from school." Neil said.

"Did you go to school?" Roger enquired, playfully. Janine hit him with her handbag.

The taxi dropped them in Casemates, a large square which narrowed down to Main Street on the far side.

They followed others who were walking down Main Street.

The shops were closed but the bars were open as were the fish and chip shops. They walked the length of the road until Roger realised Janine was getting tired.

"It's further than you think. Could we find a pub for a sit down? We can see the rest tomorrow in the daylight."

Neil went to make a sarcastic remark until he saw him looking down on Janine.

They had reached the Governor's Residence with its large cannon outside. They found a pub, The Angry Friar, but just at that moment a fight had broken out and someone was being forcibly evicted. They turned and walked back the way they had come.

"I saw somewhere on the way up." Janine said. Her feet were seriously aching.

Someone directed them to the plaza, which turned out to be John Macintosh Square, opposite which a road was called Irish Town.

"That's more like it." Neil said. "There's bound to be a decent pub down here."

"At least I now know where the Police Station is." Roger said as they passed it.

They found The Clipper and Janine was quite forcibly found a stool to sit on.

"They were given their pints, a shandy for Janine, and Neil watched for when the barman was free. He leaned on the bar. "Is this an army pub or a navy pub?" He asked.

"What's it to you."

"More than you know, Pal. Say the wrong thing and you'll certainly lose my custom while I'm here. Army or Navy."

"We get both but there's never any problem. The Irish visitors usually find us and we get the odd naval officer. What are you?"

"Ex-army and I'd prefer to drink with the navy. Thanks." He raised his glass and moved away.

"What was that about?" Janine asked.

"Just checking there wasn't going to be a problem if I come here again."

"You know too much about the habits of the army." Roger suggested.

"We all do." Neil answered darkly.

Saturday morning Janine made sure she had flat comfortable sandals for walking. She wasn't going to be caught out like that again.

When the boys left her, she made her way into the first clothing shop she came to. Mostly they were loose caftan type of dresses, not what she would wear. Most of the skirts were rather old fashioned and plain, the style the older women were wearing. It took until she came to a wider area near a church that she found a more modern shop. She had been drawn to this the evening before, mainly due to a dress in the window. Someone was asking about it. Bother. She went in anyway and rooted around on the clothing rails and found a pair of white trousers, the ones that only came just below your knee like in the films. She picked out a Tee shirt with an interesting design and a skirt which swung when you twizzled. She had never dared buy one in England.

The shop assistant came to speak to her and she mentioned the dress.

"It was not in her size." She said.

"Oh Good!" Janine exclaimed. It was in her size.

Now what else did she need. A bathing costume. She picked a blue one with straps that came from around the bust, over the shoulders and crossed at the back. The shop assistant asked if she was interested in a bikini. At first she was horrified, until she saw the turquoise one with black spots. It had a frill around the waist and the straps were thin and black with two on each side. It was all edged in black. If she never wore it, she still wanted to have it.

She'd only gone there for the dress. It was mainly blue in various hues with the odd touch of pale pink among the swirling pattern. Cut in panels, the sides fitted close to her figure until around her hips where inserts made it lay in folds around her knees. The top had an oval cut out below the neckline which appeared daring without actually showing anything. The sleeves were loose and unmade, reaching almost to the elbow. But it was the silky lightness of the material that made it shimmer as it moved. Janine was entranced with it.

With her paper carrier bag she started back down main street. She didn't really have any light skirts and she had never worn jeans. Perhaps if she found another cotton skirt it would be cooler than those she had brought, in spite of it being late in the year, it was still very warm to Janine. She found a paisley cotton skirt and unexpectedly, a broderie anglaise blouse which looked different when she put it on. It had a square neckline which was unusual.

The shopkeeper was waving a brightly coloured top at her. She didn't really want it, it was much too bright for her. He was telling her to try it on. She supposed she would call it a peasant style, with an elasticated neckline that you could pull off your shoulders, and elasticated at the waistline. Somehow the warmth and brightness of the light changed how she felt, and she felt daring. She bought it. If she only wore them on holiday, at least it would make it memorable.

Now to find The Clipper and somewhere to sit down. This heat certainly made her feet ache.

Neil and Roger walked alongside the boats moored in the harbour. Most of them were leisure craft, made for a day out. Some were larger and looked occupied.

"Hello." Roger said to the man washing the deck.

"Hi there. On holiday?"

"Do we stand out?" He enquired.

"You are a bit on the white side. Just arrived?"

"Yes. We came by boat, it's the first time for us."

"Small or large?"

"What, the boat? A cruise ship, the Wilhelmina."

"I thought it was only elderly rich ladies who went on cruises." He laughed.

"There were plenty of those." Roger retorted.

"Why the boat? Usually you young ones are in such a hurry you like to fly out."

"Spur of the moment decision, I suppose. A friend of ours came by boat recently and we decided to follow suit. Do you live on it?"

"What, the boat. Well it used to be a pleasure craft only, but Franco keeps closing the border to traffic and we were obliged to leave the car outside and it was stolen, so we sold up and live here."

"Isn't it cramped?"

"Bijou, we call it. It certainly prevents you from accumulating clutter." He laughed.

"I think the boat my friend was on was rather larger than that. We were wondering if they called in here to refuel."

"Johnjo could tell you that. He's the harbourmaster and deals with all the visiting craft."

"Thanks. I don't suppose you met Percy?" He speculated.

"Not that I know of. I could have been at work."

They wandered along in the direction he had indicated.

"I don't think we should mention Percy to this Johnjo." Neil speculated.

"Probably not. He might know the Abrams quite well. That man might know them, but we never mentioned the name of the boat."

A cruiser was pulling in to the dock to refuel and a wrinkled and sunburnt man was shouting orders at them.

"That could be him."

They sat on bollards and watched from a distance.

"Do you think that's the size of the Mandarina? How big do you think she is?"

Someone had come out from an office and was helping to refuel, leaving Johnjo free to move away in their direction. Roger and Neil walked towards him.

"You looking for me?" he asked.

"If you're Johnjo, then yes. The man on the boat down there said you were the person to ask. What size is that boat? It looks hug

"Hundred and five feet, thirty two metres, she's a beautiful craft."

"She's bigger than the Mandarina III then. She's only about ninety feet, we were told. It would need more crew, wouldn't it?"

"You know the Mandarina?"

"No, we were hoping she was here when we arrived. Did she stop here when she refuelled?"

"She only refuels on the way out, they stop on the way back. How do you know about her?"

"A friend of ours was on her."

"Sergio?"

"No, the Abrams and Sergio invited him. I don't know if he actually came."

"There was only the three of them, as usual, so it doesn't look like he did."

"Pity. Thanks. Be nice to own something like that, wouldn't it." Roger said to Neil, conversationally.

They wandered back along the harbour and out onto the street.

"Like we expected, he wasn't on it. If they had reported an accident, Johnjo would have known."

"Where do we go next. Into Spain? We've only just arrived. We're supposed to be on holiday."

"I wonder if anyone official can give us any ideas of how to search. Spain is a big place, and he could have been found in Portugal. It's going to be a long trip, Neil."

"And probably a pointless one. We could be viewing endless bodies of drowned tourists."

"I think I'll go to the Police Station and ask if they know about anyone missing, or a body being found in the area. Perhaps the Guardia would ask them if they had lost anyone."

"I'll go and find Janine. The guy in the Clipper said some Navy went in. They would be the ones to ask."

"Once we've ticked the boxes officially, then we can decide where we go from here."

They walked up Irish Town, Neil going into the Clipper while Roger continued up to the Police Station.

"It's busy, where do we go now?"

"Fish and Chips." Neil announced.

"It's hardly private there." Janine said.

"What is there to discuss?" Neil muttered.

"What were you talking to the bar tender about?"

"When the Navy men came in. He suggested about half six, seven when the visitors have gone back to their hotels and there are few people about. There's often a naval lieutenant comes in before he goes on duty. He must be on nights."

"Night patrols?" Roger suggested.

"That would be helpful. I'll go back tonight and see."

"You don't need us with you, do you?"

"No. Probably best if I am on my own."

"Good, we'll save you some dinner." Roger joked.

"It won't take that long." Neil insisted.

Neil leaned on the bar in The Clipper and watched everyone who came in. Some were holiday makers already drunk from the hotel bars. A few were off duty forces personnel, off for a night out. One or two were watching, like Neil. Either they were on duty and watching for problems, or just trying to keep out of trouble. Some looked like junior officers who preferred not to drink in the officers' mess where they would be outranked.

Neil caught the barman's eye and ordered another pint. He indicated one of those at the far end of the bar. "Navy?" The bartender nodded.

Neil took his pint and made his way in his direction.

The man was in his late twenties and had 'navy' written all over him, and yet he was dressed in dark clothing apart from the epauletts on his shoulders.

"Hi." Neil said.

The man looked at him in surprise.

"Navy?" Neil said.

"Why?"

"Why am I asking? I'm looking for a naval officer who could give me a little assistance."

"You've got the wrong man." He went to walk away.

"We've lost someone."

"Go to the Police." He said.

"Not here, from a boat somewhere between Lisbon and here."

For a few moments the man never moved.

"What about him? What do you mean 'lost'?"

"He was on a boat in Lisbon but never arrived here. He was missing when they refuelled."

"Can't you ask the boat owners when they come in next time."

"No. They can't know we are asking."

The man looked closely at Neil as if deciding whether to just walk away. "Who are you?"

"I'm a private detective looking for someone who is missing."

"If the authorities find out who you are you could be in trouble."

"Not as much trouble as Percy."

"How do I know I can trust you?"

"Check with MI5." Neil murmured.

The man blinked. "Ah. Give me your name. It might be best if this goes no further. I'm not sure my superiors would approve."

Neil took out his official badge which gave his name and photograph and the name of the company, Williams, Mathers and Phelps.

"Do you need the special phone number for England?"

"I think we know how to contact them. How do I contact you, Mr Phelps?"

"I'll come back the same time tomorrow."

"It's Sunday tomorrow. I'll wait outside for you. You are cautious."

"I need to be."

"Are you alone? There are three names on your badge, are you all here?"

"Yes."

"Don't inform anyone else. It could be dangerous."

"It usually is when we get involved. We're supposed to be on holiday."

"Then go and enjoy your holiday and I'll see what information I can find."

"Thank you." Neil held on to his hand as he shook it.

"Ah. Lieutenant Southam."

"Night patrol?"

"Well I suppose you are a private detective."

"The dark clothing gives you away."

"Does it really. I must be more careful in future, but I am due on duty soon. I'll see you tomorrow, Mr Phelps."

CHAPTER SIXTEEN

It was Sunday and most of the shops were closed, so they decided to sightsee. The alternative was to stay by the crowded pool and be jostled by the tour visitors who had no outings arranged. Most were determined to turn themselves into lobsters as quickly as possible and were fighting to get the best position. Even the Catalan Bay beach was full.

With many others, they queued to ride on the new cable car installed to take visitors to the top of the rock to see the spectacular views. There were paths to walk, views in all directions, including down the east slope towards their hotel which was hidden by a complex of sheets of iron installed to catch water. The original pathway snaked down the mountain, past the apes sniffing the fumes from the car exhausts, past Saint Michael's Cave, eventually arriving down at sea level.

"I'm glad we walked down rather than up." Janine said. "Where do we go now?"

"To eat?" Neil suggested.

"Neil!"

"I suppose it is gone lunch time. Let's find a café." Roger decided.

It was impossible to talk through any decisions with people around them, so they found their way back towards the hotel and went onto the end of Catalan beach where it was now in shade and they could sit apart from others.

"You can't go alone tonight." Roger insisted. "I'll need to cover you, even if he notices me."

"The Clipper is closed, it's Sunday. He will see if you come."

"There must be others walking around, even that late."

"He probably won't have any information anyway." Neil decided.

"Think back to what he said, Neil. He intended to phone MI5 and check you out. Why would he do that if he had no information. He must have known something or he would have just refused."

"Please be careful." Janine insisted. "How do we know they won't arrest you and hand you over to the authorities. Or worse, what if they know the Abrams."

"If anything happens, Janine, you must phone Lionel urgently for help. You are our lifeline." Roger looked at her with such a serious expression and she understood how important it was for all of them to know how to react.

They walked up to the nearby Caleta Palace and saw Janine safely inside, before setting out to walk to town. Using taxis all the time left them open to anyone knowing where they went.

Roger walked ahead and passed the Lieutenant as he leaned nonchalantly against the front of The Clipper. Neil followed a little behind.

Southam nodded to him as he arrived.

"You're very trusting, coming on your own." Southam said.

"Am I. What did you find out?"

"That you are who you said you are. Actually, the man said 'So that's where they are. I should have realised they wouldn't give up'.

Neil burst out laughing. "You spoke to Lionel."

Southam grinned at him. "As for your missing man, I do have information. This is confidential, you understand."

Neil nodded agreement.

"We are not allowed any contact with Spain, nor them with us, unless it is official, and long winded, and includes the Governor and possibly a government minister. But there are times when we need to pass information. The Guardia from Tarifa asked if we had lost someone from a boat. At the time we knew of nobody. A message has been sent concerning your enquiry. They want to see you and see what identification of him you have."

"How do we get there."

"We take you. If you go yourself nobody will speak to you. Can you be ready tonight, say eleven thirty?"

Neil lifted his arm in a half-hearted wave. A few moments later Roger joined them.

Southem looked at him. "I gather you are Williams. Phelps can fill you in. You need to be here dressed in dark clothing at eleven thirty. Will you be missed if you don't return until tomorrow night?"

"We'll need to tell Janine to cover for us."

"We'll fetch you back the same way we take you. We can't be seen to wait and you need to be there during daylight. Like I told Phelps, take whatever you have on the man with you."

"Fine." Roger agreed. "We'll go and have dinner and warn Janine."

At exactly eleven thirty, Lieutenant Southam arrived to lead them into one of the admiralty buildings and through to the naval dock where a patrol boat waited.

"The men know little about you, but enough to be discreet. It will be the same ones who pick you up tomorrow night. If you've never been to Spain before you're in for a shock. Try not to show it."

Roger hunkered down as low as he could. It being dark he was pleased he couldn't see the deep dark water they were speeding through. At one point they were off loaded onto a small rock or jetty where another patrol boat waited to pick them up and take them to Tarifa. A police car met them and took them to the Guardia headquarters, which resembled a large warehouse building. They were deposited in a room with men of various ages, none of whom spoke a word of English.

Eventually someone indicated that they should make themselves a coffee. Men came and left, discussed or argued, wrote reports and drank coffee at the same time as the television blared continuously.

They weren't being ignored, it was just that there was nobody yet who knew what they were there for.

"I suppose we had to come in the dark, but obviously whoever wants to see us is on days."

A young man came in, still buttoning his shirt, grabbed a cup of coffee, downed it in one, and left.

"They must live here." Neil said.

"That's why it's so big, I suppose."

"They seem to run on strong coffee. Don't they eat breakfast?"

Eventually a man came and indicated them to follow him. They were taken to a canteen and given another coffee with something like greasy pastry rolled in sugar, they called it churros. He leaned forward and spoke a few words.

"You have?"

"Yes." Roger replied. "I have a photograph."

"Fotografia?"

Roger nodded.

There was a television blaring here as well, they were showing a re-run of a bullfight. Well they presumed it wasn't live at this time in the morning.

Men stopped to talk to him, they presumed they were asking about them.

By the time someone came to take them, they were both riveted to the television.

There was no television in this room, only a serious man.

"You have fotografia?" He said in broken English.

Roger pulled the photograph out of the inside pocket of his loose jacket and put in on the desk. The serious man opened a file and laid out a serious of photographs.

He pulled one photograph to the side of theirs. There was no argument, this was Percy, one of his face alive, the other of his face pale and dead.

He turned another with a picture of his skull and its deep depression. "Asesinado" He said.

"Asesinado. Oh, assassinated." Neil said.

"Yes. Murdered." Roger agreed.

"Who he is?"

Roger turned over the photograph to show his name and date of birth. "Percy Blenkinsop. A civil servant. He worked for the government."

"Govnent? Gobierno. A functionario de la Gobierno."

"That sounds about right." Roger nodded.

"Percy Blenkinsop." It didn't sound the same when he said it.

The officer picked up the phone and spoke to someone.

"You go."

A couple of Guardia came in and encouraged them to follow.

"Where are they taking us?"

"Who knows. Back to Gib, possibly."

"No, we're being taken back in the dark. It's all arranged."

The car was hot and the men were smoking which added to the lack of air as the open windows channelled the smoke into the back of the car.

They drove up a hill, saw a lookout point above them, came back down to sea level and pulled up amongst pine trees.

They indicated that they get out.

"I hope they don't intend to leave us here." Neil muttered.

"It is seriously hot." Roger agreed, his light jacket now over his arm.

The sand was hot and soft as they were led through. The cover was a blessed relief until they came out onto the beach beyond. There were few people around, but then it was still fairly early.

"If it's this hot this early, how bad it is in the middle of the day in high summer?"

They were walked down to the tide line where the guardia pointed to the edge of the sea.

"Man." He said, which seemed to be all the English he knew.

"This must be where they found Percy." Roger said. "Percy Blenkinsop." He told them.

They both nodded but never tried to copy him.

"Man" One of them copied how he must have looked, laid on the sand with his eyes and mouth open.

"Thank you." Then thought of the little Spanish he knew. "Gracias." Roger said.

The men nodded and started back towards the car to Neil's great relief.

On the drive back they stopped at a restaurant by the roadside and drank another coffee and ate more 'churros'.

"I think these are fried." Neil said. "They're very greasy."

"And very sugary." Roger added. He didn't have a sweet tooth and they were not to his taste.

It was late morning now, and they had been awake all night. The heat was making them sleepy.

They were almost back in Tarifa, but at a place with strange white walls.

One of their minders stayed in the car, the other took them to one corner and pointed to a particular square in the honeycomb edifice. It had a rough concrete slab with a date scratched in it and a word they didn't understand.

"Where is this?" Neil asked.

"Cemetario"

Roger pointed to the slab. "Percy Blenkinsop?"

The man nodded.

"He's buried here? I wish you had your camera?" He indicated taking a photo of the grave. The guardia nodded. "El Capitan." And he nodded again.

"It looks like they have a photo of the grave. Gracias." He said. "They appear to stack their bodies in walls here."

They were taken back to the Guardia Civil building and left in a more comfortable room, with chairs they could relax in and sleep. And they did sleep, even through the obligatory constant television programmes.

The sound of people moving around brought them awake. A guardia they recognised fetched them to see 'El Capitan' again.

He appeared to be thanking them and offering them photographs.

Roger realised. "Proof!" He said. "He is saying something about needing proof." The captain nodded. "La Prueba."

"El barco?" He asked.

"What does barco mean?"

"El barco?" He could have been driving a car.

"I think he wants to know which boat. What was it called."

"Why?" Neil asked.

The captain took out his revolver which made both of them step back, but he patted it. "El armamento?" They looked at each other. Roger nodded.

"Yes. Probably armaments."

"Gibraltar."

"They think they are smuggling arms to Gibraltar." How does he say this. "No, they were still loaded when they left. Very low in the water." He makes the same driving movement trying to show them going beyond Gibraltar. Bending to show the boat was low in the water.

"El nombre del barco?" he asked.

"El barco? The Mandarina III." Roger turned to Neil. "I wonder why they need to know the name of the boat?"

He telephoned someone and they heard the name Mandarina being given. Shortly after, someone arrived with a folder of more photographs.

They both looked at them. "These are photos of the Mandarina III going, low in the water and coming back, riding high. It looks like they monitor the shipping through the straits."

Roger nodded to say it was correct. Going she was low in the water, coming back she was high.

There was nothing they could do to correct their impression that they were taking arms to Gibraltar.

They were returned to the comfortable room until much later, when their minder came and took them to the canteen for dinner. The soup tasted like mint, the main course was hoops of rubber and there were no vegetables, but there was plenty of fresh bread. And more coffee. Although most of the men seemed to be drinking wine.

When darkness had fallen, they were taken back to the patrol boat to be transferred to the naval vessel and returned to Gibraltar.

Lieutenant Southam led them silently into the naval building on the wharf at Gibraltar.

"Successful?"

Roger pulled out the photographs and showed him the face, the damaged head and the grave.

"What now?"

"We decide how to proceed."

"What was the boat?"

"Why?"

"I want to monitor them."

"MI5 will do that."

"They aren't here."

"It could be dangerous."

"I'm aware of that. We need to protect everyone else."

"I suppose. The Mandarina III."

"Don't worry, I won't spread it about."

"Thanks."

"Take care walking back. Do you have far to go?"

"The Caleta Palace."

"I can't offer you a lift."

"We'll cope. Thanks for your help."

CHAPTER SEVENTEEN

Janine felt rather lost when she woke up on the Monday morning. She had been alone before, but only in her own home. This was a strange place, a long way from safety, and brought back memories of her time alone on the army camp.

'Pull yourself together girl,' she thought.

Breakfast was taken late, when most of the tour companies had removed their charges to show them Gibraltar, en masse, or take them on boat trips to show them Gibraltar, from afar, or to show them the beaches of Spain that they are not allowed to stop at. Some of the busses take them to the border and they walk through to join Spanish busses waiting outside for a long drive to the Alhambra.

A few families had not left and, like her, were staring out at the Mediterranean Sea and the tankers waiting to dock with supplies, while they ate their very English breakfast. She wondered if the captain and crew of the tankers were looking out at them eating their breakfast.

The maid had made her bed while she had been in the dining room, and she had opened the window. She could hear the sea, but only similar to on the boat. The tide must have covered the pebbles.

With no desire to wander around on her own, and nothing she especially wanted to see, she decided to take her book and sit by the pool. It would be her first opportunity to wear her bathing costume without the others being there to make comments.

Wearing her costume with the swirly skirt over the top, she took her book and purse and made her way to the poolside. There was not much room to sit by the shallow end where the steps went down into the water, so she was obliged to sit further round.

The book had been bought on board the Wilhelmina. It was 'The Casebook of Sherlock Holmes' and she was trying to work out what happened before the book said, pitting her wits against Sherlock Holmes, or at least Sir Arthur Conan Doyle.

As the sun grew too hot for people, they sat under the umbrellas or nearer the shallow end of the pool, as it lost the sun early. Lunch was a fancy sandwich and a cold drink from the bar. She went back to her room for a while, then she returned, only to find the best places were now taken and she was obliged to sit further round. When she grew too hot she stood up to fetch a cold drink, she was not prepared to shout and wave for a waiter.

There were some older boys there who would have done better playing on the beach. They were getting in everyone's way, charging around and deliberately bumping each other.

As Janine made her way around the deep end of the pool to reach the bar, the boys cannoned into her and she fell, yelling in terror as she did.

The water was warm, but she landed on her back and sank, waving her arms ineffectually. It took a few moments for people to realise that she was not swimming, that she couldn't swim.

A man of around forty dived in and pulled her up. Willing hands pulled her onto the poolside, but she was in shock and full or water. She was turned over and pumped to clear her lungs and make her breathe. Her saviour had made it out of the pool and took charge.

"I'm a doctor." He said.

When she was breathing better and trying to get up, hands helped her. "Sit her down on the chair." The doctor said. He took both her arms to propel her backwards to the chair and Janine erupted, kicking and flailing, knocking the doctor back into the pool and no doubt causing him more than a few bruises which would ruin his holiday snaps.

It was obvious that Janine was not in control. A kindly lady offered to take her to her room and gently escorted her. A young girl, probably her daughter, went to fetch her book and purse and check the doctor was okay.

Janine was laid on the bed shaking, wrapped in her dressing gown. The kindly woman sitting on the chair watching her. When the young girl arrived, she was obviously upset.

"Lucy, can you go and ask if they will bring a cup of tea, and perhaps a roll and butter. It would help to soak up any water she swallowed and settle her stomach."

"Did I hurt him?" Janine murmured.

"He's going to be covered in bruises." The girl Lucy remarked.

"I'm sorry. I didn't mean to hurt him."

"He was only trying to help."

"That's enough, Lucy. Go and get a drink for her and apologise to the doctor. She obviously didn't mean to hurt him. She was frightened."

When Lucy had gone, Janine cried a little to relieve the tension inside her.

"Don't get upset, dear. It wasn't your fault. I used to be a nurse and I've seen reactions like that before. Someone hurt you in the past, didn't they? A man." She said gently.

Janine couldn't bring herself to turn over, she just nodded her head.

"I'll explain to the doctor. You were very effective with your feet. Has someone taught you?"

"The Police." Janine murmured.

The nurse's eyes opened just a little wider. If the Police were involved, then what happened was rather more than a random attack.

A maid arrived with a tray containing a plate with a roll, a pat of butter and a cup of tea with a bowl of sugar lumps.

Janine made the effort to sit up.

"I am sorry. At least I didn't black out this time."

"Have you done that before?" She resisted asking for more details. The girl was obviously still upset.

"Was that a long time ago?"

"The last time was only a couple of weeks ago. He intended to shoot me." Janine suddenly realised what she was revealing. "I'll be okay now. I think I'll just stay here for a while and rest. I am sorry to have been such a nuisance."

"You aren't the nuisance, it was those two lads. Their parents should have better control of them in such a crowded area. Are you here on your own?"

"No, I have two friends with me, but they're out for the day."

"And you didn't fancy going. Well at least you won't be alone later on."

"Thank you so much. I wouldn't have done that for the world. You will apologise for me. I'll look for him later, but I doubt he'll want to see me."

The nurse patted her on the leg and left her to drink her tea and eat her roll.

Nurse Brody did find the doctor, surrounded by a knot of indignant well-wishers.

"As a doctor, I would have expected you to recognise the reaction to a man taking both her arms and pushing her backwards."

Most of them stopped and looked between the two. "She was very effective with her feet." He said.

"The Police trained her. At least you didn't have a gun." She said quietly. She left the group to their silent thoughts.

Janine just wanted to be left alone to sleep.

The nurse woman had opened the windows for air and because the room was too cold for her and she was shaking.

The air is warmer now and she is covered with her dressing gown. She drifts to sleep. Someone telephones and asks if she wishes to come to dinner, but she says no.

Dinner is being served and everywhere is quiet. Someone is talking on the walkway below her window.

"Johnjo will recognise them. He's pretty sure they are staying here. He's seen them since in the town."

"We could push him off the balcony and make it look like an accident."

"Not with two of them. Johnjo thinks they might have a female with them."

"How nice for me, someone to play with." The other man jokes.

"Not for long, Sergio." Janine sat up in panic. They are talking about them.

Someone arrived to speak to them.

"I can't stop long, I'm about to serve at table."

"This won't take long. We just want you to see if there are two young men, possibly with a girl, in the dining room. If so, someone is waiting at the front door to speak to them. If you show him which table, he will take it from there. We'll pay you."

"Why do you want them?"

"They were interested in our boat and we just want to give them a trip in it."

"Possibly back to England." The voice of Sergio cut in.

"I think I know who you mean but they're not on my tables. I have to go."

After a few seconds of quiet, the voice of Sergio said "Do you think he will?"

"He will. He wants the money. Johnjo knows his man. We'll go and wait in the car."

Janine laid for a short time and began to realise that she is frightened of the water because she doesn't want to die now. She has so much to look forward to in the future. What if Roger is in danger! She is part of this agency, it's about time she acted like it.

What should she do? They need to leave, but the boys are not there. She can pack her bag and be ready to go, but she has no idea what time they will return. She needs to be there when they get back.

A maid knocks on the door and comes in, not realising she is in there.

"I'm sorry." She goes to leave.

"No. It's OK."

She sits in the chair while the maid turns down the bed. She has a bunch of keys with a tag for level -1. To get into the boys' room she needs a key. She could push a note under the door, but what if they don't see it. She definitely needs to get into their room.

She watches as the maid goes into Neil and Roger's room, then follows her to reception where she gives her keys to the receptionist, who puts them in a cabinet on the wall behind him, and gives her another set. The cabinet has a key in the door at the moment, all the maids are turning down the beds during dinner.

Above the cabinet are the pigeon holes where your room keys are kept when you are out and where they hold your passports. She needs to get their passports.

Janine waits on the top step of the stairs from their rooms. She can't quite be seen from reception but she can hear.

It appears the waiter hasn't come. A man has come to the reception and asked for him.

"Johnjo, what can I do for you?" the receptionist asks.

So that's Johnjo from the marina.

"I need a quick word with Marcelo. He is going to point somebody out to me."

"He's serving dinner!"

"It won't take a second. Perhaps he can come between courses?" He said, hopefully. "I'll wait outside."

Johnjo disappeared to stand with a cigarette under the awning outside the front door. The receptionist lifted the flap and swung the door open, closing only the flap as he went to ask

Janine watching and listening from the top of the stairs, hears when the coast is clear, slides under the counter, opens the cabinet and takes the bunch of keys for level -1, then reaches up for their passports. Crouching down under the counter again, she leaves to stand on the stairs until her heart slows down.

Janine packed her suitcase and checked the room was clear. Not knowing where they would go, she was wearing her new paisley skirt and the white broderie anglaise blouse. She carried a cardigan in her bag for during the night when it was colder.

Careful not to be seen, she took her suitcase and let herself into the boys' room. She could hardly pack for them, they would need to change when they came back.

The windows were open, so she lay on the bed with the light off, listening for any further conversations. Eventually she fell asleep. She awoke when it was full dark, closed the window, pulled the curtains and put on the bedside lights. Nobody should be able to see the light if they came looking in a boat.

At three in the morning, two very tired men crept silently down the stairs and negotiated their key into the lock.

There was a light in the room. Neil indicated Roger to stay back while he went inside. Then waved him to follow.

Janine lay asleep on one of the beds, her suitcase on the floor.

Roger touched her arm and she jolted awake.

"What are you doing here, what's happened?"

"The Mandarina III is back and they are looking for us." She recounted what she had heard.

"We need to leave." Roger asserted.

"How do we check out in the middle of the night without someone thinking it odd." Neil said.

"Why do we need to check out?"

"Passports, keys." Neil reminded him.

"I've got our passports." Janine said.

"Well done! If we make the reception think we have a taxi coming to take us to the airport I doubt anyone will make a fuss, I don't expect they'll notice we've gone."

"I need a shower and change of clothes, we both do. It won't take long to pack."

"Why do you still carry a backpack rather than a suitcase, Neil?"

"Habit, I suppose. Where are we going? Or rather, how are we going. Are we going to fly back?"

"It's too early to fly back." Roger said. "Lionel needs more time and the Abrams are still here. They could find out where we were if we went by plane?"

"That's true. We can disappear into Spain and nobody will know where we are."

"Including us." Janine added.

Roger stopped in the middle of packing.

"Why were you in your room with your window open when dinner was being served?"

"It's a long story. I'll tell you on the way."

"No, now."

"Some lads pushed me in the swimming pool, the deep end. A doctor fetched me out and I attacked him."

"Why?"

"He had hold of my arms and was trying to make me sit down, I think. Someone who used to be a nurse brought me back and sat with me. She opened the window."

"Really, Janine." Neil said from in the shower. "We can't leave you on your own without somebody attacking you. There must be a sign over your head 'I'm on my own'."

"Lots of people are on their own and they don't get attacked." Roger muttered.

"They were unruly boys. I shall know next time not to sit near the pool."

"You could just learn to swim." Neil suggested.

"Stop talking and get a move on. We need to get out of here as quickly as possible. If they know where we are staying there may be someone watching, we need to be very quiet and very careful."

CHAPTER EIGHTEEN

ontrary to what he had told Neil, Lieutenant Southam had informed his senior officer what he was doing. Without his authority he could not have phoned MI5. However, Captain Deveraux had been out to dinner on the Tuesday evening when the lieutenant had reported for duty, so it was Wednesday evening before he had any chance to speak to him.

"Was it worth it, Southam?"

"Yes, sir. They had photographic evidence. Should we phone MI5 and tell them?"

"I imagine your private detectives will do that. Don't spoil their success."

"No. Sir.

"You'll need to be careful tonight, it's already getting rough. The weather people say there's a storm tracking our way from the South Atlantic. It's due to hit in the early hours. We've put a limit on the size of shipping going through until it runs its course. It'll be choppy enough to put small craft off for a while even when its blown itself out."

Southam went to check out the weather report and organise where to patrol before it became too dangerous.

The storm hit earlier than expected, just after midnight. It came up the African coast and was funnelled into the straits by the Atlas Mountains, causing the winds to rise. Once it cleared the narrowest part of the straits at Tarifa it dissipated, easing as it passed Gibraltar, blowing itself out completely before daylight. The following morning there were only the odd remnants of clouds in a clear sky and the air felt fresh and clean.

It had been a quiet night for Lieutenant Southam. Much of it confined to the building as they listened to the winds howling outside. He was glad it was not that night they had needed to fetch the two lads back. He wondered if they had phoned in their information.

"They think we lost a boat last night." The night patrol was just going off duty and its replacements had arrived.

"We weren't called!" Southam said.

"It was beyond Tarifa. They were stupid to go. The afternoon watch tried to get them to turn back."

"Timms never said anything when we came on duty. Did Tarifa pick them up?"

"No idea. Duty Officer got a radio call saying they were holed and sinking. They've tried to contact Spain but there's no news. I think they may have put up a flare so we can but hope. It depends if Tarifa could get out, the storm was much earlier than expected."

"Any idea what the boat was?" He asked.

"Ask the duty officer, he'll know."

The Lieutenant went to the notice board to see the name of the missing boat, but there was nothing there except a list of boats in port on the day before. What caught his eye was the name 'Mandarina III' on the list. Did Phelps and Williams know they were in port? He ought to warn them.

Southam was reticent about going to the marina. No doubt they would be in shock over the lost boat. Johnjo would have seen them leave, probably advised them not to go. In the afternoon, before going on duty, he went to the Caleta Palace Hotel and asked for Phelps.

"I am sorry sir. They are no longer here." The receptionist sounded annoyed.

"When did they leave?"

"We are not really sure. If I may say, we are getting tired of people looking for them."

"There have been others?"

"Yes sir. If you will exc…"

"Who? Describe them to me."

The man stared at him. "I don't even know who you are."

"I'm sorry, I am not in full uniform. I am Lieutenant Southam of the Royal Navy and I need to contact them urgently."

"So did those who came in the other day."

"Which day?"

"I really don't know, Lieutenant. I wasn't on duty at the time."

This was out of his remit. He needed to report to Captain Deveraux as soon as possible.

On his return he did call at the marina. Johnjo came forward immediately.

"Any news?"

"I've not been told anything, Johnjo. Can I ask you about somebody? A couple of young men asking about the Mandarina III. Have you seen them recently?"

Johnjo never answered for a few moments and Southam presumed he was thinking.

"Nobody came and asked me anything." He said, curtly. Then turned and walked away in a way Southam thought rather out of character.

The loss of the boat was the talk of the mess when Southam arrived. The problem was the name of the missing boat. Mandarina III. He needed to speak to the Captain urgently.

"*Is* it urgent, Lieutenant?"

"Yes, sir. I went to speak to Phelps and he isn't there. They can't tell me exactly when they left and I was not the only one looking for them."

"They could have friends, Southam."

"No, sir. The boat the body came from was the Mandarina III, which has been in the marina. Phelps told me he asked Johnjo how many were on it when it arrived on the way out and he said the normal three. I've just spoken to Johnjo and he denied having spoken to them."

Deveraux walked to his window and stared out at nothing while he thought.

"They were warned not to go, but they were in a hurry and thought they could beat the arrival of the storm. Why? I think we need to phone England."

"Yes, sir."

"Use the secure line and I'll authorise it."

A very shocked Lieutenant made the phone call to England and went to report back.

"They will phone as to which plane he will be arriving on."

"This is serious, Southam."

"Yes, sir. Rather more than just a missing young man, sir."

"So it seems. No doubt he will want to speak to you when he arrives. I think it may be best if I second you to work with whoever arrives. You're excused duty. Get some sleep if you can."

"Thank you, sir."

Before he went back to his room, Southam went back to the marina and spoke not to Johnjo, but to those who were living on their boats. If anyone had any information it could be useful.

Lionel himself arrived Friday morning on a British Airforce VC10 at ten fifty, he looked strained. Southam, in full uniform, stepped forward to meet him.

"Are you the Lieutenant I spoke to?"

"Yes, sir."

"This is a bad business."

"Yes, sir. I'm to take you to the Governor's Palace, sir."

"Is he involved?"

"Not that I know of, sir."

"What does he know about it?"

"Not a lot." He said candidly.

"Then tell me what you know as we drive. I take it this is our transport?"

"Yes, sir."

"How did you get involved?"

"Phelps spoke to me in a pub." Lionel gave a small smile. "He was looking for a missing man. When he mentioned it could be a body, I took note. We had been told by Tarifa of a body found on a beach, but we knew of nobody reported missing. I took the two of them in the night patrol launch and fetched them back the following night. We are not allowed contact with Spain, unless it is through the Governor and a minister or high official."

"So this was off the register?"

"Yes, sir."

"Does the Governor now know?"

"I have no idea if he has been told."

"Then it may be best if my presence is not known. Who does know?"

"Captain Deveraux, my superior officer."

"I suggest we find him. This is not an official visit and I am not prepared to spend my time making small talk with officials."

A message was sent to the Governor's Palace that their information had not been correct and the civil servant who had arrived was there for a few days holiday, not an official visit. If anyone questioned the unscheduled arrival of a British Airforce plane they were not liable to be given a reason.

Captain Deveraux confirmed that no information had been given to the Governor's Palace. When the call had come the information had been relayed to the senior officer on duty who had put in place the protocol for a visiting dignitary.

"First the hotel, I think. We need to know who knows what."

The manager was phoned and a meeting arranged for the afternoon. It was attended by Captain Deveraux, Lieutenant Southam and Lionel, who took his own notes.

"When did they leave? They must have checked out."

"That is the problem, they were there one day and the next they were not there."

"Are their keys missing?"

"No, the keys are here, although their passports are gone."

"When did anyone last see them?"

"Their waiter barely remembers them. They must have been here over the weekend. There was some unpleasantness on the Monday when somebody pushed the girl into the swimming pool and nobody realised she couldn't swim. It appears her reaction to the man who saved her was most violent."

Lionel took a deep breath and let it out slowly. "Do we know who pushed her in?"

"Just some boys, I believe."

"Not done on purpose?"

"Why would they?"

Lionel turned to Southam. "They came back Monday night?"

"Yes, sir."

"When did anyone start asking questions?"

"Monday or Tuesday, I can't actually say. One of the receptionists said Johnjo from the marina was looking for someone and one of the waiters was supposed to speak to him."

"Do we know who it was?"

"He hasn't turned up for work since. It's a nuisance."

"Can I speak to the receptionist, please?"

"Which one, the one who spoke to Johnjo?"

The receptionist was very vague. Johnjo wanted to speak to Marcelo who was supposed to be pointing out someone, but he never came. He sent the message that they were not in the dining room, so he couldn't show him."

"Monday or Tuesday?"

"Probably Monday, but I really couldn't say which day it was. Marcelo could probably tell you but he hasn't shown up for work since then."

"Do you have an address for this Marcelo?" he turned to Captain Deveraux "I suggest someone calls to check on him."

They returned to Naval headquarters in silence.

"Who is Johnjo?"

"The harbourmaster of the civilian port." Captain Deveraux replied.

"You say he denied having spoken to them."

"Yes. sir." Southam answered.

"I think we need to speak to him."

Southam went to stand and arrange the driver.

"Here, I think. Not in his own environment, Captain."

"Of course." The Captain agreed.

"Will he come willingly?" Lionel asked.

"Oh yes." Southam almost interrupted. "He'll think it's something to do with the missing boat."

"Is there any news?" Lionel enquired of the Captain.

"No, sir. But we aren't actually allowed to contact Tarifa direct."

"International politics can be very difficult."

When Johnjo arrived he expected to be given information and looked hopefully between those sitting at the desk. The tall thin man he had never seen before was the one who spoke.

"Johnjo is an unusual name. Is it your actual name?"

"No." He answered "I thought everyone knew. There were quite a few Johns and Jones in our ships company, and as my name is John Jones, I got called Johnjo."

"I understand you visited the Caleta Palace hotel recently and asked a waiter to point out somebody? Is that correct?"

Johnjo looked shocked.

"I was asked to find where they were staying and we'd checked everywhere else."

"Why did you need to find them?" Lionel could sound very menacing.

"Someone wanted to offer them a passage back to England."

"That someone was Eli Abrams or Sergio?" He suggested.

Johnjo blanched. "Yes."

"Why did you tell Lieutenant Southam that nobody had asked after the Mandarina III."

Johnjo looked sick, now. "I don't know."

"Did they find them?"

"I don't know. They spent two days searching. I started to worry why they were so adamant. They checked everywhere, then suddenly they said they were leaving. I told them not to go, there was a weather warning, but Sergio said they could make it to the deeper water before the storm hit." He turned to the Captain "Is there any news?"

"None, but then we have no official contact with Spain. Can you contact anyone?" He said to Johnjo.

"Not that the Guardia will talk to."

"Did you see anyone but the Abrams and Sergio go on board at any time?" Lionel asked.

"No, sir."

"Then it seems you can be of no further help."

Johnjo was rather upset and being dismissed so summarily with no information.

"You think they were on the Mandarina?" Captain Deveraux asked.

"Why would they go?" Lieutenant Southern said.

"They may not have had any choice."

"Are they in danger?"

"If they were on the Mandarina, it appears they are probably already dead and if not, then I don't give them much of a chance. We have at least three dead bodies so far and who knows about this Marcelo."

"If I may say, sir." Lieutenant Southam started hesitantly. "I went back to the marina and spoke to the occupants of the boats moored there. Apparently, there was an argument on the Mandarina late on Tuesday night, it sounded a very heated one. Someone saw the older man go to the telephone on Tuesday evening and one questioned why they were filling fuel cans when they had already filled up. Oh, and the woman went shopping and bought a great deal of food."

"You have no idea who was arguing?"

"No, sir."

"I don't like the sound of that. Not at all." Lionel shook his head.

"Can I ask, sir." Captain Deveraux said "What they were doing that was so secret?"

"You mean with their heavily loaded boat going and their obviously empty boat returning. Illegal arms."

"Do you think Johnjo would have known?"

"He may not have known what, but he is ex-navy and would have noticed a boat low in the water who returned very high in the water."

"Can I ask, sir." Southam said hesitantly. "Do – did they work for you?"

"No, Lieutenant. Not that I wasn't looking at the possibility of recruiting Williams. He has always been the leader and organiser. What a waste. I am surprised you haven't heard of them, from their book at least. The army are still smarting over their exposure of what happened. We had to put out a warning about taking reprisals against them. Unfortunately for them, somebody from the Government needed a private agent and thought of them. Anyone less dedicated would have given up when they handed it to us. These three were too conscientious."

Lionel suddenly looked extremely old and weary.

"I will fly back this evening if you can arrange a flight for me. If you hear any news, please let me know. Do you expect the boat to be found?"

"No. I very much doubt it. She was holed and sinking when she radioed. I doubt she would have survived for anyone to get to her in time. Anyone in the water would stand no chance in those waves."

"Why the extra fuel in cans?" Southam asked.

"The telephone call to England, Lieutenant. They must have realised they had been discovered and intended to make a run for somewhere. Could the boat have made it to South America?"

"At a pinch, in good weather. But it's doubtful." The Captain answered.

"Any ideas of how she was holed?"

"Not unless there was something loose in the engine compartment or storage."

"Or someone." Lionel suggested darkly.

CHAPTER NINETEEN

Carrying their suitcases, they climbed silently up the stairs to reception. Janine went first and checked the receptionist was not the one on duty when she took the keys.

Neil asked if the taxi had arrived and the Receptionist went out of the front door to check. Janine threw the bunch of keys onto the floor below the cabinet as if they had fallen out, and stuffed their room keys in the pigeon holes.

There was no taxi there, of course, so the receptionist phoned for one while they waited outside.

"Why are we going to the airport?"

"We need to change money into Pesetas. They should have a bureau de change there."

The airport was open but silent. They tried the border but the kiosk was closed, so they waited at the airport. Gradually people started to arrive and they were able to ask. There was a flight due in at six thirty and the bureau would be open then, so they sat and waited in silence.

It was starting to get light when they made it through the border to Spain.

The road outside was empty, so they crossed into the small town they could see, and found themselves in a rather unkempt area that might, at a pinch, be called a square. There were people there, but none looked as if they would speak English. They were leaning against the wall outside the door of a small bar. Some were inside drinking coffee. When some women arrived, they went to the bar and came out with tickets in their hand.

"I wonder if they're waiting for a bus?" Janine said.

"If so, what are the tickets?"

Janine went to one of the women, she would not have dared to go to the men, and pointed to the paper in their hands. "Bus?" she made the sign for driving.

The woman nodded. "Autobus." She said. Then pointed to the café.

"It looks like you buy tickets from the bar."

Roger went in and emerged a few minutes later with three tickets.

"We must remember that. You need to buy your bus tickets before the bus comes. Perhaps they don't trust the drivers with the money. Or they think they might get robbed."

"I wonder where the bus goes?"

"He never asked which bus, so I would say, wherever it goes, that's where we're going." Roger joked.

The bus was basic, old and uncomfortable. It rattled on the straight, leaned when they turned a corner and crunched when he changed gear, but it took them to Algeciras. To a bus park where everyone dispersed in a matter of seconds, there was no information, no office and nobody to ask.

They wandered down a road where many of the passengers had gone.

"We need a map." Neil said.

"Ask at that kiosk." Janine suggested.

"What are they selling?"

"Tickets of some kind. Do they have lotteries in Spain? It says Lotteria over the top." He went to the kiosk to asked. "Map?" Roger said tentatively.

"They won't understand." Neil went to say.

"Mapa." The man said, then he pointed down the road. "Tabac."

"Gracias." Roger said. "Down here we look for 'tabac' whatever that is. Perhaps somebody will show us."

"I'm thirsty." Janine said. "Can we get a drink in that café."

"Don't eat the churros." Roger muttered.

"They weren't that bad." Neil said.

They dumped their bags by a table and went to the counter.

"How do you ask for a drink?" Janine queried.

The bar tender was watching them with amusement.

"Caliente o frio?" he asked. When they looked bemused he lifted a cup from the top of the coffee machine and put his other hand into somewhere under the counter. He put the cup on the counter. "Caliente." He said. Then he put a bottle of orange drink on the counter. "Frio." He said.

"Frio." Janine said with a big smile.

"Coffee." Neil said and pointed to the cup. Roger nodded his agreement.

"Grasias." He used the only word in Spanish that he knew.

Janine took her bottle and sat at the table with Roger while Neil waited for the coffees.

"We'll be fluent in Spanish by the time we leave. Hot and cold, map and when we find it, we'll know what tabac is."

Neil came with the coffees. "Look over the road. There's a shop with a sign saying Tabac. It looks like it sells cigarettes."

"That would make sense, if tabac is a tobacconist."

"Why are the coffees so small?" Janine asked.

"They just are. The Guardia Civil seem to live on the stuff."

"They have cakes of some kind." She went to the counter and pointed to the glass case with various cakes inside. Holding out one of her notes for him to take."

"Magdalena." He said.

"Oh. That's what they're called. Magdalenas." Having picked up the word from Roger she said "Gracias."

"I'll go and see if they have a map." Roger said, standing up.

"Mapa." Janine reminded him.

Someone came in and ordered a Magdalena and a coffee and came to sit at a table nearby.

"His coffee is much bigger." Neil complained.

"It looks milkier." Janine said, trying not to stare.

The man seemed to understand as he was trying not to laugh.

Roger was back in a very short time. He was armed with a small map of Algeciras and a folded map of Spain.

He laid the map of Spain on the table and began to unfold it.

"So, where do we fancy going?"

"I want a coffee like that man's." Neil muttered.

"So ask him." Janine said. "I think he can understand us."

Roger turned to speak to him. "Excuse me, do you speak English?" He asked.

"I do indeed." He said in a very English voice. He was obviously amused.

"What a relief!" Janine exclaimed, and everyone laughed.

"What is that coffee.?"

"Café con leche." He said. "What you had was café cortado. It's what the locals drink. It's unusual to drink milky coffee in the morning." He looked at the map. "Where are you planning to go?"

"We have no idea. North, somewhere up the coast where we can have a quiet relaxing holiday away from England."

"Quiet! On the Spanish coast. It's full of British holidaymakers.

"If we go by bus won't somebody remember us." Janine suggested.

"Bus! Like that bone shaker we came on. No thanks." Neil said.

"Is there a train?" Roger asked.

"Not up the coast. Where do you actually want to go?" The man asked.

"Somewhere for a holiday where we can easily get a plane back to England when we want to. Where would you go?"

"Me? I'd go to one of the islands, like Ibiza."

"We'd need to fly to get there."

"No, you can go by boat from Denia." He pointed to an area between Alicante and Valencia. The boats go from there."

"How do we get there?"

"I suppose there may be a coach rather than the local autobus. I can't imagine it would be comfortable, all that way in a hot bus. If you go by train you need to make sure you know where you change or you could accidentally end up in France. There are no trains that go up the coast because of the mountains. That's why you need to change so many times. By the way, take something to eat and drink on the train, there's no telling how long it will take and they don't have such things as restaurant cars."

Exploring further down the road, they found a bread shop with a variety of bread. They picked several kinds of rolls as being easiest to carry, plus some cakes that were displayed. A general food shop, which seemed to sell everything from wine to baby clothes provided them with bottled water and a fizzy orange each. Then using the local map, or mapa as Janine insisted, they found their way to the station.

"I hope all that shopping hasn't made us miss the train." Janine worried. Her bag was bulging with all the food.

They wanted to go to Alicante, Roger kept saying, but he didn't understand the man behind the grill. A backpacker from Sweden came to their rescue and explained that he was saying where they were to change. Roger gave him his notebook and asked him to write down the station names, then he paid for three tickets, no, **three** tickets, he kept holding up his fingers until he understood.

The train left at ten fifteen.

"Is it only that time. It feels like midday." Janine said.

"That's because none of us have had any sleep." Neil complained.

"We can sleep all we like on the train." Roger said.

"So long as we don't miss the station where we change trains." Janine reminded everyone.

"In that case, we need to sleep in shifts and make sure one of us is awake at all times."

They went to find the platform, but the backpacker called them back. They must punch their tickets before they get on the train, or the inspector will fine them, they were told. Roger looked down at the tickets.

"There's no date on them. I suppose you could use them twice if the inspector never came."

They sat on the platform, out of the sun, and waited patiently.

"Roger, why are the tickets only for Alicante? I thought we were going to Denia?" Janine asked.

"If anyone manages to follow us the ticket seller might remember us and tell them where we went. From Alicante we can go by train or bus to Denia, and anyone will be searching Alicante for us."

"Elementary my dear Watson." Janine joked.

"Where did that come from?"

"I'm reading Sherlock Holmes."

It was almost seven in the evening when three hot, tired and dusty people arrived at Alicante station."

"A bus might have had air-conditioning." Neil moaned.

"I doubt it." Roger muttered.

First Roger found someone who could speak English, a little, and asked about the train to Denia. There wasn't one, only a tram around Alicante. He says they should have gone to Benidorm, it was nearer. Go by autobus.

Now he needed to know where the bus ran from. Details and timetables came with the tickets from a ticket office at the train station.

"Not what I was hoping." Roger said. Neil just grunted.

The bus would take a long time, going through villages and stopping everywhere. It was too late for that night. They would be better taking the early bus in the morning.

"We need somewhere to stay." Janine said.

They found a Pensione, something like a boarding house, not far from the station and sank into rooms, collapsing on the beds. After washing and changing, there was no shower, they went looking for somewhere to eat.

"We need to plan for tomorrow." Roger said.

"Plan for what?" Neil asked in a bored voice.

"If we have gone to all this trouble to avoid detection, then we need to make sure nobody on the boat crossing can remember us. With three of us together we do stand out."

"Where do you intend to leave me?" Neil muttered.

"Nowhere, Neil. Don't be like that. We just need to be careful. I suggest that two people won't be noticed as much as three. If, say, Janine and I buy tickets as if we are together, and you buy one as if you are on your own, then we won't be noticed. Janine, if you take a change of clothes and change on the boat, when we land in Ibiza you can land with Neil, looking different, and I can be the single one."

"Can I just finish my dinner and go to bed." Neil said.

"That's the best idea yet." Roger agreed.

Early morning saw them drinking café con leche and eating magdalenas in a bar as they waited for the bus.

It was a long, hot journey, through villages and small towns. It stopped in Benidorm where most people alighted and more entered. It was lunchtime when they arrived.

They rushed to the boat station to buy tickets. The notice board showed the next sailing to be two o'clock and they needed to hurry to board in time.

"I'm not sure which will be worse, the heat inside or the sun outside." Roger said.

"I'd rather stay outside, if it's all the same with you."

"You're in a bad mood, Neil. For the first part of the trip you're on your own, so you can go wherever you like."

They were sat on a bench, Neil, a short way away and facing in a different direction to give the impression they weren't together.

A coach was unloading passengers who were being hurried as they collected their cases from the driver. They swarmed onto the deck, herded by a woman in a uniform.

"Over here, please. Are we all here? Can everyone hear me?" She never waited for anyone to reply. "You are free to move about the boat as you wish, all I will say is, don't leave your cases unattended. We will meet here at around five thirty so I can give you instructions for where to go when you disembark. The sun will be hot, so please take precautions and make sure you drink a lot. Thank you ladies and gentleman you are free to leave."

"She didn't tell them where the toilets were or how often they should go." Neil whispered

Janine had a fit of the giggles.

Once they were sailing, Neil disappeared inside and Roger and Janine endeavoured to find a place out of the sun, shaded by the cabin.

"I'm going to get a drink. Do you want one?" Janine asked.

"A bottle of water would be good." Roger had to curb his desire to protect her to the point of preventing her from moving around freely.

When she returned she was carrying a bottle for each of them.

"Neil's at the bar drinking beer. I hope he doesn't get drunk."

"He's not stupid. I doubt he'll drink too much. If he does it will probably come up again before we leave the boat."

"It isn't that rough, Roger."

"I know, but even so there are a few who are looking a little green around the gills."

When Neil reappeared, he came to sit close to them, put his rucksack at the side of Janine's case and leaned forward.

"Stick with the group." He muttered. "I'll tell you later."

Roger moved away to sit opposite and Janine took her bag and disappeared inside.

The group were now beginning to assemble and Roger watched them for something to do. Occasionally he looked over at Neil to see if Janine had reappeared. Janine had been wearing her white broderie anglaise blouse with her paisley skirt, her cardigan hung over the bag for if it was too windy, which also camouflaged the colour of the bag. Her shoes were open toed with a small heel. She had looked like his girlfriend or wife. Wishful thinking.

What he first saw was the look on Neil's face and his mouth saying 'Wow!'. What he next saw was Janine, but not as he had ever seen her before. She wore flat sandals, white, close fitting, three quarter trousers with a slit to the knee, a highly coloured blouse which was pulled off the shoulders and showing a large amount of neckline. He hair had been pulled up into a pony tail on the top of her head, and she was wearing makeup and bright red lipstick.

She went to sit with Neil and Roger felt a lump inside him. He picked up his case and moved away where he was out of sight of them. He put his suitcase on end and sat on it, staring out at the sea.

He was jealous. He knew it, and he had to decide what to do. Neil had never shown any interest in Janine beyond friendship, and they had been friends for years. What if he had suddenly seen her in a different light? What if she preferred him? He breathed deeply to calm himself. When they had somewhere to stay, he must talk to Neil and see what his intentions were. They had lived together for long enough for them to hold a sensible conversation over this. One thing he would not do, he would not pressurise Janine in any way. It would be her decision who she chose and he would abide by it, even if it condemned him to a lonely future. He would need to decide if he could remain friends with them without it tearing him to pieces inside.

The woman had arrived and was waving to everyone to pay attention.

"Are we all here?" Roger doubted they were but she never waited for a response. "Keep together when we leave the ship, we're walking a little way down the harbour wall to where there are boats waiting to take us across the bay to the Argos. Make sure you keep your suitcase with you at all times, you will not be able to come back to retrieve anything and it will be difficult for me with so many of you to look after. When we reach the hotel, you will need your passport and booking form to assist us to locate your rooms as quickly as possible. Dinner is being served at seven, so please make sure you find the dining room in time. There will be a welcome party in the lounge bar after dinner when you can ask any questions."

As soon as the walkway had been lowered, the eager group, terrified of being left behind, pushed their way off, in some cases using their cases as battering rams.

Neil, with Janine walking beside him, followed close behind. Neil carried his rucksack on his shoulder and Janine was carrying her own case. Neil should have been carrying it for her, Roger thought.

They processed eagerly down the harbour until their tour guide forced her way through and stopped them. She made a count which didn't include Neil and Janine, or Roger who had hung behind.

There were two tourist boats with canvas awnings, standing waiting.

"Can you all listen." She shouted. "Because of the amount of luggage it will take two trips across, so those who arrive first will need to wait for the rest of us. Is that clear?"

There was a general muttering and she began to load people onto the first of the boats. People refused to go without their partner or insisted on going because their family member was already on board. In all the confusion, Neil and Janine managed to get onto the second of the boats.

As it pulled away, Janine looked back at Roger, still standing on the harbour wall and she appeared to be in panic, talking to Neil agitatedly.

Once the first boat had unloaded it started back for the next group, and Roger managed to get onto this boat. There were still some people waiting, older couples who would never dream of pushing in, but were prepared to wait in line for their turn.

Once on the strip of land between Ibiza bay and Talamanca bay, Roger looked around for Neil and Janine. Neil was a short distance away by an oversized garage without a driveway, which turned out to be a very basic bar.

"Hello you two. Trust you to find a bar, Neil."

"We can't arrive with the group or there might be a problem." Was Neil's reason. "How long should we wait?"

"Not too long. Dinner is a seven and everyone will be eager to find their rooms. We don't need a tour guide or receptionist, we need the manager or whoever deals with bookings."

Neil finished his drink, Janine leaving her glass with a small amount in it. She had pulled up her top until it was a normal round neckline, and she had taken down her pony tail. She looked more like the Janine he knew. She still had some makeup on, but her lipstick had mostly been left on the drinking glass.

"We'll investigate this place later." Roger suggested.

Roger went into the hotel alone. There were more than enough people still discussing rooms, the receptionist had left it to his colleague and the tour guide to sort things.

"Do you have any rooms free." He asked.

"You are with the tour company?"

"No. We need two rooms for at least a week."

He excused himself and went into an office, arriving with the manager.

"Our rooms are contracted to the tour companies. What kind of room were you looking for?"

"There are three of us, two male and one female and we require two rooms for at least a week."

"Like I said, our rooms are contracted to tour companies, if you wanted to apply to them they may be willing to accommodate you. We are not in a position to let you have any of their empty rooms."

"The tour company have a tour operator who organises, they have booked outings and flights, we want none of that, just rooms for a holiday." He insisted. "If you have no rooms then can you recommend somewhere near."

The man appeared to consider his request and decided that would be a loss of revenue. It was a recently opened hotel and they were trying to make a name for themselves. What if these were from another company who might book rooms in the future.

"We have …" He seemed to be unable to find the word in English. The tour lady was still in reception and he called over to her. Explaining in Spanish what he was trying to say.

"He is trying to tell you that he has a suite of rooms free but they will probably be more than you can afford." The last part was probably added by her.

"How many bedrooms and how much do they cost?"

"Two bedrooms, a bathroom and a lounge." She answered while the manager fetched his book and wrote a figure on a sheet of paper.

It was expensive, but it was private and secure. He didn't have enough pesetas on him, so he asked him to wait while he went to the door and called Neil and Janine. Between them they found sufficient to pay for a week on half board, bed, breakfast and evening meal in what turned out to be a very upmarket suite of rooms on an island in the Mediterranean where, with luck, nobody would ever find them.

CHAPTER TWENTY

"Why did you say to stick with the group, Neil?" Roger asked.

"I heard them talking. The tour wasn't full, a family had needed to go home, so there would be spare rooms. They were discussing who paid in a case like that. They also said it was a bit remote, so I thought it would be suitable."

"It is more than suitable?" Janine purred as she stretched out on one of the sofas.

"I guess you get the bathroom and double bed." Neil said as he looked into the second room. "This one has twin beds."

"How do we get to the bathroom from our room?" Roger murmured as he checked doors. He found a door into the bathroom from the lounge area. "This is how."

Neil had taken his backpack and thrown it on a bed. He was checking doors for wardrobe space. "Hey, there's a shower room." He called.

"She didn't mention that." Roger said.

"Jealous cow." Neil muttered.

"She said we couldn't afford it." Roger added.

"Like I said. She's a jealous cow. Probably has a tiny room somewhere over a restaurant. Takes it out on her holidaymakers with their en suite rooms."

"I'm glad we're not on her tour." Janine said.

"Probably her charges will feel like that by the end of the holiday."

"Dump the cases and get a move on, dinner is at seven and we don't know where the restaurant is yet." Roger insisted.

"Just follow the noise." Neil suggested.

People were milling around finding tables and staff were trying to steer them. This table had insufficient seats for their family, this had too many and they didn't want to share. Most of the tables were set for four people, so couples were going to need to share.

Roger waved their room key at the hovering waiter and they were propelled down the room to a table in the window, which various staff had been defending from insistent people.

"I like this." Neil grinned. "We get preferential treatment."

The waiter spoke only a little English, but it appeared this was their table and would be set for three.

Janine was giggling as she listened to the mutterings of people on adjoining tables as to why their table was larger for only three of them. They would find the following day that there was a reserved sign to save the staff having to remove people.

"What a lovely view, or it would be if only it was still daylight." Janine was looking over the water but the light was fast fading.

"If this is our table for breakfast then we'll see it in the morning. We need to find out what time breakfast is."

"I'm sure Neil will do that." Janine laughed. "I can't see him missing out on food that's paid for." She gave a sideways glance at Neil who at first was annoyed, then realised she was joking and rolled his eyes.

"Are we going to the meeting in the lounge bar afterwards."

"Count me out." Neil muttered, darkly.

"Perhaps one of us should, if only to see what to avoid. Perhaps there will be some useful information. If it turns out to be just that woman being bossy then we can leave. Are you going to that bar?"

"Yes. Hopefully not everyone will find it."

"I expect most of them to stay in the hotel. It is rather plush." Janine suggested.

"And you like plush?" Neil asked.

"Why not. I've never had plush before. I could get used to it." She laughed.

Friday night was 'Sangria Night' when there would be musicians. Saturday night was 'Beach Party Night' outside where there was another bar. This was the goodbye night for those leaving on Sunday.

Roger and Janine left when the information went on to the outings and how to join them.

They found their way out to the beach and walked along the sand. Janine took off her shoes and carried them hung on her finger.

"It doesn't seem real." She said.

"It does seem too good to be true." Roger agreed. They found their way over rough ground to the road and across to where Neil would be sitting with a pint or bottle, whatever was available. As they crossed the rough areas, Roger took Janine's hand to prevent her from slipping. Once over, he never let it go.

"What do we do tomorrow? Swim?" Neil said, eyeing Janine.

"I hate to say it, but we used all our pesetas paying for this. One of us needs to go to the bank to change some English money."

"Don't the hotel change it for you?" Neil suggested.

"They change travellers' cheques, but I'm not sure about money. I doubt they'd give the best exchange rate."

"I'd like to go into Ibiza tomorrow." Janine chimed in.

"In that case, you two can go to Ibiza town and I'll go and swim. You don't really need me, do you?"

"No, Neil. So long as one of us has a passport for the bank it should be OK. You might need to go if we need more. It depends if they stick to this fifty pounds limit."

The following day saw Roger and Janine on the little ferry across the lagoon to Ibiza town.

"Just as a point of interest, why do you want to go?" Roger asked.

"I want a pen and paper."

"For something particular?" Roger queried.

"You know I've been reading Sherlock Holmes. Well in it, Watson writes up all the cases they deal with. I thought, being as I was often in the office with little to do, I should write up all our cases. Well the large ones, at least."

"To publish them, like we did our case?"

"Not necessarily, although if I did, I would need to change the names of the people or I could be sued."

"It's certainly a brilliant idea. You could publish them as a story and nobody would know they were actually real."

"That's what I thought. I want to make a start and write things that have happened so far. The longer I wait the more details I may forget. There will be times during the day when I can sit quietly in the lounge. I wouldn't do it if I had an ordinary room, one of you would be knocking on the door all the time to see where I was."

"It would be a memory, that's for sure."

"I think we should take a momento back from here. Something to remind us of this place. In fact, something from every special place we visit."

"You feel this place is special?"

"Yes, Roger, I do." She looked up into his face with real seriousness.

"Good, then we look for something while we're here. It saves us dragging around the place at the last minute. You do realise the house will become full of souvenirs."

"I was thinking of things we could put on the wall that would remind us, when we were at home. I don't fancy things that get knocked and broken and need dusting all the time. Besides, I wasn't thinking of everywhere we went. Just something to remind us of a special case we solved."

The bank changed Roger's money with no problem, especially as he had his passport to prove who he was. They never endorsed his passport as England would have done.

As they wandered around the shops, it was very apparent that Ibiza was very different to England. They did cater for the tourists, but mostly it showed in the number of bars, some of which were only open in the evenings.

They found a stationary shop, something they would not have expected. All it sold was paper and writing books for school, pens and pencils, ink and address books, oh, and sheets of wrapping paper.

Janine rummaged through the pile of writing books.

"These are all like maths books. Look, Roger. They're ruled into small squares. How are you supposed to write on that?"

"Let's see if we can make the assistant understand us." He held up the book and made as if writing. The assistant nodded to him. He shook his head and made a sign for paper with lines on it. For writing. She held up a small book she made notes in and it was made of tiny squares, any line being the one to write on.

"Oh dear. I don't think I can use that. Perhaps they have plain paper books."

"They have writing paper for letters." Roger said pointing to sheets on the counter.

"That's no good. I need a book where I can keep everything together." She found a drawing book but it was rather unwieldly for writing."

"You would be using the table, so it might work."

Having decided that would have to do, she chose some biro pens. The assistant, who seemed to have eventually understood what she meant, found a lined writing book similar to England and waved it at her.

"Yes!" Janine said. It was very thin, so she tried to make her understand that she wanted more. She held up three fingers, not two, that could be misinterpreted. The woman went through a pile of books on the shelf behind her and eventually found two more.

They left with a parcel wrapped in paper.

"I'm exhausted." Janine said.

Roger was laughing. "Next time you need to take it with you from home."

They went to a café and sat for some time watching the antics of some of the visitors in the street outside. They appeared to be still drunk from the night before.

"We have such restrictive drinking laws in England that young men like that go overboard when they come on holiday." Roger noted.

"I'm glad you're not like that, Roger."

He didn't know what to say, so he just smiled at her.

The shop they found was not just for souvenirs, it sold jewellery as well. It was all metal and the labels said 'Toledo Steel'.

"Would you like some earrings?" He asked her.

"I don't think so. I don't have pierced ears and the clips are uncomfortable. They do have plates." She said, wandering over the peruse the display on the wall.

"Now that *would* be a momento." Roger said. She could hear the wistfulness in his voice. He was staring at the section of wall with Toledo Steel swords on it.

"Then you must have one." She said decisively. "It would look good on the wall at the back of the desk in the office."

"It would, wouldn't it. Do you think Neil would approve?"

"Neil would prefer it to be a gun, but as that is not possible, I'm sure he would approve. Buy it, Roger."

They made their way slowly back to the boat and across, just in time. The boat stopped during the afternoon siesta for two hours.

Neil wasn't there when they got back, so they opened up their parcels and laid them on the table.

"Can we afford room service?" Janine asked.

Roger laughed, "Of course we can. Do you want a drink?"

"Yes please. The heat doesn't make me hungry but it does make me thirsty."

"Tea?"

"Do you think they do it.?"

"I would imagine so, although it may not taste the same as in England. The water's different."

He phoned down for drinks, then they took a sofa each and relaxed. This was going to be a stress-free holiday after all they had been through.

Or so they thought.

At five o'clock, Neil appeared. His nose was bloodied and his knuckles had blood on them. He looked battered.

"What the hell happened to you!" Roger exclaimed.

"A small contretemps."

"It doesn't look small. They won."

"Actually, there were three of them and it was probably a no score draw."

"What actually happened?"

"They were well oiled and getting rough with a girl. I think she came on the boat with us, probably about seventeen. They wouldn't take no for an answer so I said it louder, with my fists."

"We're supposed to be having a quiet holiday, Neil." Janine heaved a sigh.

"I didn't start the fight. I only got between them and the girl. Once one hit me I defended myself. I don't think they expected it."

"Your jeans are torn." Janine said,

"I know, one of them had a knife."

"Did he cut you?" Janine sounded concerned.

"He cut himself." Was all Neil said. "I'm going to get a shower."

A while later, Neil appeared looking clean and normal, but he was frowning.

"He sliced open my pocket, presumably to get at my wallet, but I didn't have any money."

"A good job. He went empty handed."

"Actually, no. They've taken my official pass."

"What!"

"Are they staying here?" Roger asked, sitting up.

"Yes, I think so. They were taunting me about having a special table."

"Then they are. We need to find their room numbers."

"What for?" Janine asked.

"Because we need to do a little late-night burglary and get Neil's pass back. MI5 will not be over the moon if that turns up somewhere it's not wanted." Roger insisted.

They slid into their seats at the dinner table, aware that they were being watched.

"I take it there were others there at the time." Roger muttered.

"Half the hotel, I would say." Neil answered.

A middle-aged man was making towards them.

"Now comes the trouble." Neil muttered.

"I'm sorry to disturb you, but my daughter assures me that you are the young man who defended her this afternoon."

Neil looked embarrassed. "They were drunk." He said.

"They were rather more than drunk, young man. I can only thank you for your assistance. Were you hurt?"

"The odd bruise, nothing to worry about." Neil said.

Roger stood and spoke to him.

"It may sound strange, but we would like to know the room numbers of these thugs. If you could point them out or make a note from their room keys it would help."

"I hope there won't be any trouble."

"Not if they give him his property back." Roger growled.

"They took something?"

"An official pass. Any help you can give us in finding their rooms would be gratefully accepted. I doubt they will respond to a little word in their ear after dinner. They don't sound the type."

The man looked troubled. "I wouldn't like anyone hurt."

"If they take my pass back to England and try to use it, they're likely to get more hurt than they expect." Neil growled.

The father was true to his word and enlisted all those who had witnessed the incident to assist. The answer came from someone who had the misfortune to have the adjoining room.

The sangria night began in the dining room at nine. The tables had been cleared and laid in lines with white tablecloths and a glass jug of red wine full of fruit. Fruit was draped over the edge, dangling into the wine.

People fought to get a table at the front, where they could see and be seen. The three concerned agents looked for a table at the back where they could watch for trouble.

The girl was there with her parents and turned to smile at Neil as they passed. Neil grinned at her.

"Well there's Neil's entertainment organised for the week." Roger joked.

Neil made no reply. Now that was interesting.

They were not at the sangria night. The boys delivered Janine back to the suite, just a little inebriated from the wine, and went looking. They were not there. Someone thought they had gone into Ibiza to a night club. The one person they did not ask was the receptionist.

They could hardly ask for two keys, so Neil went out the back and came in the front door and asked for the most probable key. The receptionist never challenged him, he just handed it over.

The room was a mess. There were suitcases open on the bed as if they had never unpacked or were packing to leave. They began with the bedside cabinets and moved on to the suitcases. They opened everything and searched everywhere. There was no sign of the pass.

"What if he's still got it on him."

"He'll rue the day." Neil growled. "It could be in the other room. How do we get that key?"

"I go out the back and round while you give back this key and I ask for the other. I doubt they'll be back until late."

The pass was displayed stuck on the mirror like a trophy.

"They'll know we've been in."

"Tough."

"We need to keep an eye on Janine or they could go for her."

"They're more likely to go for me." Neil said.

"Oh, I don't know. They never beat you and there were three of them."

"Let's get out of here."

They returned the second key and wandered into the lounge bar where people were still drinking. The girl was there with her parents and friends they had made. She came over to Neil.

"Hi." She said. She was a little embarrassed.

"Hi. Are you OK."

"Fine." She leaned on the bar at the side of Neil.

"Do you want a drink." He asked.

"I'm not allowed." She put her hand to her mouth. "I had some sangria."

"You're not drunk, are you?" Neil joked.

"Of course not." She insisted.

"Fizzy orange?" He asked. She nodded.

"You're very strong." She began.

"Not especially." Neil said.

"Dad said you must have trained."

Neil looked at her, then turned away a little embarrassed.

"I was in the army."

"Oh, I see." As if it explained everything. It certainly didn't explain some of the moves Neil had been taught by the Police.

Roger excused himself to go upstairs and check Janine. The last thing he wanted was to play gooseberry.

The following day they spent on the beach. Fiona joined them when the three bullies, bearing the bruises that everyone presumed Neil had inflicted on them, appeared swaggering along the beach trying to outstare everyone. When they went in the sea and horsed around everyone near moved away or came out to lay on their towels on the sand.

Roger found it funny that Fiona was treating Neil like a Guardian Angel. The funniest part was that Neil seemed quite willing to take on the role.

They only had one day to survive. Word was, they were going the following morning on the Manchester flight and that they came from Bradford. Neil would accept that from their accent. He and Janine both had a northern accent which he had never tried to remove. He had grown up in Ripon with Janine and her brother. He was aware that Roger had made a note of their addresses in his book.

Dinner saw them at their round table for three. Fiona was with her parents and it was obvious that the three guys were staring, not at Fiona, but at their table. From Neil's point of view, it looked like they were focusing on Janine.

"Are we going to the Beach Party later?" Neil asked.

"We can if you want. What do you want to do, Janine?"

"It could be fun. I suppose they have music, not just drinking."

"If everyone going home tomorrow gets drunk, they'll have a dreadful journey." Roger joked.

When Janine went into her room to change, Neil collared Roger.

"We need to keep one each side of Janine, tonight."

Roger looked at him in surprise. "Why especially?"

"Those three were looking at Janine and making sneering jokes." Neil informed him.

"Were they. Perhaps best if we don't stay that late, then."

"It won't hurt us to have an early night. We've had a good amount of sun today and there are plenty of days to come when they've gone home. We didn't come just to get brown."

Some people danced on the beach but it wasn't very easy. In the main, everyone just stood around talking and drinking. Neil took note of where his three adversaries were, leaning on the bar as if they owned it, making everyone reach around them for their drinks. The bartender didn't look too happy.

"Shall we go inside for a nightcap?" Roger suggested.

"I'd rather go up to the room and sit in a comfortable chair. I've not had any time to write today."

"We can get a drink and take it up with us." Neil suggested.

Neil crashed out on the sofa which converted into a bed, while Roger leaned back in a chair and watched Janine, sitting at the table writing everything she could remember.

"Do you need any help?" Roger asked her.

"You'll need to give me the exact details about Pingewood and Mountbeck, because you were the only one there."

"Neil can tell you about his trips to Barnsley."

"Am I going to put in that you found the key and went into the house?" She asked Neil.

"I thought it was just a detailed description of everything that happened, not what anyone else would read." Neil said.

"It is. I suppose the first draft should have everything in it, then I can take out what we need to if I write it up as a story."

"I didn't break in. The key was there in the front garden, I was just checking she wasn't in there in some distress."

"Well put." Roger grinned. "We'll leave you to get on with it. Ask if you want to know anything."

Eventually they all turned in. Tired from the sun and gradually unwinding from the recent turmoil, the two men slept.

CHAPTER TWENTY-ONE

Janine's brain was alert. She had started to write and her memory was working. There was no particular reason that she needed a good night's sleep, tomorrow would be a day for relaxing, just like today, except those three awful men would have gone.

She took her book into her bedroom and tried to write in bed, but it was difficult as the book didn't have a stiff cover.

It was late when she put out her light and stood by the window. She still wasn't sleepy, but putting the light on in the lounge might wake the boys. She ran her hand over the Toledo Sword sitting on her dressing table and thought about how men had used swords in the past. This one was only for show.

The moon was shining and glinting off the sea. She sat for some time just taking in the atmosphere, not really believing that they were actually there, in paradise.

Eventually her eyelids began to droop. Time to sleep. Firstly, though, she needed to wee. She never turned on the light, her eyes were accustomed to the darkness and a light would only have woken her up.

She was hearing unexpected noises, so she never flushed the toilet in order to listen, she just opened the bathroom door into the lounge. Perhaps one of the boys was up.

The noise was coming from the door to the suite where someone was trying to get a key into the lock. All of them had a key and surely there wasn't a fourth key. It must be a pass key.

Not sure what to do, Janine went back into the bedroom, picked up the Toledo sword and returned through the bathroom to the open door to the lounge. She stood in the darkness and peered out.

The door was open now and there were men coming in. They were rather unstable on their feet, but the moonlight cast onto something bright in the hand of one of them. A knife.

They were so drunk, when they whispered it was more like a stage whisper, and Janine could hear clearly what they were saying.

"She said the men were in the right and the girl in the left. I'll take the girl." He waved the knife around.

"You going to kill her and let them take the blame?"

"Nah, not unless she fights. A nice slash across her face, give her something they can see every day. Nobody steals from me!"

If she stood there and shouted it would be too late. The corridor was only partially lit, but her eyes were used to the darkness, theirs weren't.

Janine raised the sword above her head, breathed deeply, stepped out into the room and attacked with as fierce a yell as she could manage. She brought the sword down on the arm of the man holding the knife, then slashed sideways to hit the second man. By the time they had worked out where the attack was coming from, the far door had opened and the light came on, showing both Roger and Neil throwing themselves across the room.

When she could see exactly where they were, she slashed the sword sideways at neck level to cause the nearest man to take a step backwards. He grabbed hold of the end of the sword which, though not very sharp, travelling as it was, cut into his hand and made him howl.

People had come out of their rooms to complain about the noise and the night porter had been called. Several were now in the room as Roger and Neil had each pinned a man on the floor.

The one with the cut hand was backing away from Janine and her sword but was unable to escape with the people crowding around the door to see what was happening.

The wrapping paper and some of the books were still on the table where they had opened their parcels, and that included the string. Janine threw one piece of string to Roger, and the other to Neil for them to at least tie their hands.

Neil had hold of the knifeman and was pressing in places that were causing him problems, while not being in view of the people in the doorway. Roger was gentler with the larger of the three, he appeared to be the most drunk.

The night porter pushed his way through to see what was happening.

"They had a key." Janine shouted at him. "Some woman gave it to them. She said the men to the right and the girl to the left. He wasn't going to kill me unless I fought, he was going to slash my face so everyone could see."

What Neil did, Janine didn't know, but the knifeman passed out. She knew what Roger did, she could see his hand lifting him up by his crotch, squeezing as he did. That one began to wail.

"Sit on the sofa and stop complaining." Roger said, as if he was doing nothing.

A couple of the men from the doorway now came to help. It was obvious who these three were, they recognised them.

Other staff were called and the three taken and locked in a room somewhere while they waited for the arrival of the Guardia Civil.

Everyone involved gave their room number and were encouraged to return there until they were needed for interview by the Guardia.

Janine, still gripping onto the sword, sank down on the sofa and began to cry. Roger gently removed the sword from her hands and laid it on the table, then sat and put his arm around her. She turned her face into his bare chest and sobbed.

"I'll kill him!" Neil whispered.

"Don't let anyone hear you say that." Roger warned.

Neil was scrabbling around under the sofa with his hand wrapped in a towel.

"What are you doing?" he asked.

"She said he had a knife. I'm looking for it." Neil muttered.

"The police will want it." Roger reminded him.

"They can have a knife, but not this one. They can have the knife from his room."

"Why the hell did you take a knife from his room, Neil?"

"Because I've come across his type before and they never give up. He had several knives. Why would he have more than one if he didn't intend to use them." Neil answered. "For that matter, why did you take their addresses."

"I wanted to know."

"Exactly. We need to know how to protect ourselves from them. They know where we come from, and they know our names."

Roger felt Janine shudder.

People were coming down the corridor.

A Guardia Civil arrived, together with a trolley containing tea. Whoever had thought to order tea for them must have been English, tea at such a time was built in to the British psyche.

Neil had disappeared into his bedroom and returned with trousers on and a knife in his hand. He grinned at

Roger, who encouraged Janine to put some more clothes on, while he went to get dressed.

The Guardia could speak a little English, he needed to in a town frequented by British holidaymakers.

Janine managed to tell him what she had heard and how she had knocked the knife out of his hand. The Guardia was a little put out that Neil had picked up the knife, it would mean the finger prints on it would have been compromised. Still, they thought, he was going to get enough information from everyone about what had happened on the Friday afternoon when he had been wielding a knife.

They each said what they had seen and how they had reacted.

The sword was noted and would be taken away to be checked. There was little else for the three of them that night. The rest of his enquiries would be with witnesses. They could go back to bed.

Janine was quieter now. Neil had come and sat at the other side of her and she could talk sensibly to him. He was astonished at how brave she had been and how effective. Janine just wanted to forget it. The sound of his voice saying what he was going to do to her was still going around in her head.

"Have you got an asprin?" Roger asked, "If so, take one with another drink. It will help settle you.

They never made it to breakfast the next morning, but then nobody expected them to. Room service delivered them a continental breakfast which they ate in a state of torpor.

If the Guardia Civil put every drunken and violent holidaymaker in prison, it would have needed to requisition most of the island's hotels to accommodate them. Once the statements were taken, England was phoned, the Bradford Police and those at Manchester airport were warned of what had happened. What happened to them in England was not up to the Guardia. They were glad to be rid of them. The knife was sent with the flight attendants, the sword did not belong to them so it was noted and returned to Janine.

"What if they're waiting for us when we get back." Janine asked.

"They won't be. It's too soon. The English police will be all over them to begin with. It's later when they'll try to find us." Neil assured them.

When they intended to leave became a cause for discussion. Leaving Lionel enough time to deal with everyone involved had to be balanced against how soon the thugs from Bradford would come looking for them. Arriving home to that kind of reception committee needed to be avoided.

"Fiona said their tour group go home on Thursday and fly in to Gatwick. There must be room on their flight because of those missing people." Neil told them.

"I'll go to the airport and see if I can arrange flights. We don't all need to go, so long as I have all our passports." Roger said, aware that the holiday was speeding past.

"You can sus out how long it takes to get to the airport and where the bus is." Janine said.

"You could always see if that tour lady would give us a lift in her coach." Neil joked.

"Neil!" both of them exclaimed.

For the rest of Sunday and the whole of Monday, life was calm and restful. They lay in the sun, swam in the sea, paddled in Janine's case, and generally did what they had expected on a holiday like this. Roger went to the airport on the first ferry boat and was back by lunchtime with three air tickets.

Tuesday was the first sign of a problem. Fiona sat apart from them looking sad and glancing over at them continuously.

"Why is she staying with her parents?" Janine queried.

"It's like she daren't leave them. I wonder what her father has said. Perhaps he's worried she's too fond of you, Neil."

"Poor kid. She's going to have a hell of a life if he gets paranoid over every young man who pays her any attention." Neil sounded bitter.

The answer came later, when many of them went in to change for dinner. Fiona came over to them, worried about being seen."

"I'm not allowed to talk to you anymore." She said.

"Why not?" Janine asked.

"Dad phoned someone and he said you were thrown out of the army because you killed someone." She was facing Neil and was almost in tears. "You didn't, did you?"

"No, I didn't! But the army never believed me and when we proved what happened it made them hate me even more. We've had nothing but trouble from them. I bet the person your dad phoned is in the army."

She nodded.

"Forget about it, Fiona." Neil stood up and walked away.

"Why don't you find out what happened, Fiona, instead of listening to the lies other people say. Learn to stand on your own feet like I had to." Janine insisted.

Roger was more circumspect. "When you're old enough, you can make your own decisions. But that doesn't mean you can't hold your own opinions. Just don't tell anyone what you believe. Do you think Neil would deliberately kill someone?"

Fiona shook her head.

"Then that is what you must hold to. Don't let anyone say differently, and try not to get into a discussion where anyone can insist you agree with them. Just think about this, why would the army pay compensation to Neil if they hadn't lied about him?"

Neil was standing by the water with his back to them. He never saw the sad look on Fiona's face as she returned to her room.

Neil was depressed which was no surprise to the others.

"It's going to take time, Neil. Don't get so upset." Roger tried to encourage him.

"What's the point, Roger. Wherever we go and whatever we do, I'm just a liability. Janine was nearly shot because of me."

"It wasn't just because of you, Neil. You were just the main name. If you hadn't been around then he would have found somebody else who had reported him."

Janine had gone back to their suite and Roger had stayed to bolster Neil, who still stood looking across the bay but seeing nothing.

"I'll get a job somewhere like the north of Scotland where they don't know me. I couldn't even go to America or Australia. They wouldn't have me with my record."

"You don't have a record Neil."

"Whenever I fill in a form they ask what I have done, and they want a reference from the army. I'm never going to get any kind of future."

"You have a future with us. You have a job with us. Neither Janine not I would be happy if you left."

"You'd be better off without me. You're the one with the brains, anyone can do my job."

"This agency needs both of us Neil. We're both different. You're night and I'm day."

"What the hell does that mean!" Neil exploded.

"Not what you think, obviously. You were trained. The army taught you how to function in the dark. I never really learned that."

"I don't just 'function' in the dark." Neil growled.

"I know you don't, and I don't just function in the daylight, but you're better at it than me. You learned to react and I learned to think things out from what I could see. You can't think things out in the dark, you need to react, I know that."

"So what is Janine?"

"Janine is the feed, the centre. She finds us information and relays it. She's like the ops room. Somewhere we need to protect, or we become isolated. I can't do that when I'm out somewhere."

"I do OK in the day, don't I?" Neil was almost pouting.

"You do. And I'm getting better in the night because I'm learning from you."

Neil stared at him in disbelief. "What can I teach you?"

"More than you realise. You seem to think I can do anything, know everything, but that's not true. Do you know what one of my fears is?"

"I didn't think you had any."

"A fear of deep dark water."

"But..."

"But I went sailing on Pingewood gravel pits. It was a nightmare but I needed to find information. I concentrated hard and tried to ignore the water and once they gave me a rope to hold and taught me how to lean out to balance the boat I concentrated on what I was doing instead of on the dark water. At least when we were taken into Spain it was dark and I couldn't see the water. That was harder because there was nothing to do to distract myself."

"I didn't think there was anything I could teach you. I've always felt you were capable of doing anything."

"You could teach me to climb, some time."

"Anyone can climb."

"Not if they've never done any and are nervous of heights. Bournemouth is not exactly in the alps."

"You aren't really scared if heights, are you?"

"I tell myself I'm not."

"What else do you tell yourself?"

"That I'm not jealous of your friendship with Janine."

"Why should you be jealous…Bloody Hell, Roger! I didn't realise."

"I didn't intend you to. I don't want to ruin the working relationship."

"Does she realise how you feel?"

"I don't think so."

"I think it would be great. I hope you make it. We were talking, what feels like years ago, when we were driving the coast looking for boats. She's frightened of being left alone. She was worrying about what would happen in the future."

"There won't be a future without one of us. If I went it would be because you wanted her. That's the only scenario that would make me leave her."

"Can I be best man?" Neil joked.

"There's a long hill to climb before we get that far, mate."

"I'll give you all the help I can."

"Don't push it or you could make it worse. Come and get ready for dinner. Best bib and tucker, show them you are more than their prejudices."

Wednesday was spent relaxing. Janine stayed with Neil to give him all the support he needed. Roger circulated, listening to what people were saying. If this were England he would be taking names and issuing writs. He would never let Neil know, he was not in an emotional place to cope with it.

There was a goodbye party on the Wednesday night for the tour people, but none of them went to it. They packed their bags in readiness for the early start in the morning.

CHAPTER TWENTY-TWO

The coach arrived to pick up the tour party at eight thirty. Which Roger thought strange, although the idea of being directly transported from A to B in a more modern coach was distinctly appealing. The little boat across the laguna didn't start until eight forty-five, so they would be the first ones on it.

They lugged their cases up to the bus station and waited for the bus. Again, it was old, rattled and was airless. They were crammed into their seats with their luggage on their knees. They sat in this cramped position for half an hour before being deposited at the airport bus stop.

"Why did the tour people have to leave so early? We're here in plenty of time. It's not ten o'clock yet." Janine queried.

"They must be on an earlier flight. Ours goes just before twelve and we needed to be here an hour before." Roger said.

"I thought they were on the same flight?" Neil said.

"So did I." Janine added.

"We've got ages to wait. Is there anywhere for a drink?"

They found a kiosk selling water which they had to make do with. The metal seats weren't that comfortable and Janine kept wriggling around.

"Men designed these seats." She said. "You only have to look at them. You need to be tall to sit comfortably with your feet on the floor."

Neil picked up his backpack and pushed her forward, putting it behind her.

"Thank you, Neil. The idea was a good one but there's no room on the seat for me at all now."

A familiar voice rang through the building.

"If you all come this way, you will be booked in at the desk at the end, so make your way there."

She appeared to have another tour guide in a similar uniform with her and there were a great many more than had left the hotel.

Someone made a comment that the desk was not open yet.

"I am sure it will open soon."

"Has she come with them? I thought tour guides stayed here and met the planes."

"Well she did come over on the boat with them. There must have been another hotel somewhere with this amount of people."

"With another tour guide. She looks much more pleasant."

Everyone fought to be first in the queue and some of them sat on their cases.

"They must be on an earlier flight. They said our desk opens at about ten forty-five."

They sat and waited over half an hour while the tour stood wilting in the queue at the first desk, until the second desk showed a sign with their flight number on it. They took their cases and were first in the line. A sign appeared at the first desk giving the same information as on theirs.

"Is that right?" Roger asked the girl. "It says the same flight as ours."

"When the plane is pretty full we open two desks. Don't worry, you're in the right place."

They watched their cases, and in Neil's case his backpack, loaded onto a trolley ready to be taken to the plane, then they were directed through to sit in the lounge until the flight was called.

In the background, they heard the voice ringing out. "I hope you have enjoyed your holiday, perhaps I might see you next year. Have a good flight."

"She isn't going with them." Janine said.

"If they're on our flight I am eternally grateful. I dread to think of her giving orders to the cabin staff. I can imagine the pilot turning the plane round and refusing to go." Neil said.

Some of the back of the queue had realised their desk was for the same flight and was empty. They were rushing across to book in first.

The flight was uneventful. They were fed sandwiches of some kind of meat, a small English cake and a small container of orange juice. Janine wished they had given them Magdalenas. The coffee was below par and Janine said the tea was insipid. At least they were being fed.

The plane landed at one thirty-five English time, and they waited patiently for their luggage.

Roger left Neil and Janine to get the luggage and walked around to where Fiona stood with her mother while her father waited for their cases. He gave nobody any time to speak, pushing a slip of paper into her hand.

"Read this book, if they'll let you. Then you will understand." He left quickly before anyone could accost him.

It felt like they had been travelling for a week already.

"How do we get to Southampton to get the car." Janine asked.

"There could be a bus but it would take forever. We'd need to go via Brighton. A taxi would be horrendously expensive."

"We go by train." Neil decided. "I have decidedly gone off busses." He said, which caused some amusement.

The tour passengers were whisked away in a coach. The sad face of Fiona pressed to a window.

Enquiries led them to a shuttle bus to the train station.

"I'm glad we didn't try to walk it." Janine muttered.

"So am I. I have a feeling we'll need our energies at some stage today, if only to survive the journey between trains." Roger mused.

"Travelling can be extremely tiring. I can understand why some people choose to stay at home." Janine said.

"Usually because they can't afford it, I expect." Neil told her.

They had to wait for a train. The train took over an hour. They had to wait for the Southampton train on Brighton station.

"There's a café, I need coffee." Roger said.

"Good idea." Neil agreed.

The train steamed into Southampton at five thirty and they took a taxi to the car park to pick up their car, which took another three quarters of an hour as they were not expected and they had to find their car and move other cars around in order to extricate it.

They stopped on the way to shop for food, as they knew they had nothing fresh like milk and bread, and all the shops would be closed when they got home.

It was dark when they pulled into their front drive and parked the car. Roger went to open the front door and Neil and Janine unloaded the luggage. Neil locked the car and they closed the front door and breathed a sigh of relief.

"Over twelve hours travelling. No wonder we're tired." Neil said.

"It was longer than that when we left Gibraltar." Janine reminded them.

"Yes, but we were running then, not knowing exactly where we were going. At least we're home." Roger said.

"Leave the cases where they are for now, we need a drink and some food. I'll put the kettle on." Neil went towards the private area.

"I need to phone Lionel." Roger said.

"Tonight?" Neil queried. "Won't tomorrow be soon enough." He continued on into the kitchen carrying the bag of groceries.

"We need to know it's safe." Roger called after him. Thinking about safety, he locked and bolted the front door and followed Janine into the dining room, switching out the front hall light as he went.

Roger picked up the handset and dialled the London number for Lionel. Duncan answered the phone.

"Is Lionel there?" Roger asked.

"Who it is?" Duncan sounded unsure, even though this was a special number.

"Roger Williams." He said.

There was a long wait and he could hear muffled voices, as if Duncan was talking with his hand over the mouthpiece. Then Lionel's voice came on the line.

"Williams. Where are you?"

"We've just got home. And we have proof."

"I thought you were dead."

"What!"

"Lock yourselves in and don't answer the door to anyone."

"Are we in danger?"

"Not in the way you are expecting."

There was a cry from the dining room. Janine was shouting. "There's somebody in the garden!"

Roger dropped the handset and ran to Janine. A man dressed in dark clothing and wearing a balaclava was outside the window. Neil came rushing through with the bread knife in his hand.

"Get into the front." He shouted.

The window shattered as the intruder hit it with something hard and metal and he climbed in with something that looked like a small pistol in his hand.

Meanwhile, Janine had run to Roger and wrapped her arms around him. She was shaking with fear. Roger closed his arms and lifted her, carrying her into the front of the house and sitting her in one of the comfortable office chairs. Not wanting to give their position away, he closed the heavy curtains before putting on the light.

Neil shot through the middle door and slammed it closed, locking it.

"You've left the key in." Roger said.

"They can't pick the lock with the key in." Neil said. "If you turn it a bit they can't poke it out, it takes time to get hold of the end and turn it. I've shut him in the dining room and switched the phone through. I just hope he doesn't shoot the locks off."

"If he does, he'll need to reload before he can shoot us." Roger murmured.

There was a banging on the front door. Neil was nearest so he went to see who it was, returning white faced.

"It looks like army." He said. "I can't see how many."

Roger picked up the phone and dialled the Police. Gave them who they were and where they were and what was happening. They were told to keep calm and someone would be there very shortly.

Neil switched out the light.

"Now open the curtains and get your eyes accustomed to the dark. Whoever gets in first will have come from the light and we'll have the advantage."

"Against guns!" Roger said.

"There's a torch in the desk." Janine reminded them.

"Good thinking, Janine. When they get through the door, you get under the desk in the kneehole where they won't see you."

"So long as I can help watching through the window now."

"Why not. Once anyone comes in, nobody speaks." Neal said. "They'll need time to see where we are."

The pounding on the front door continued, together with the sound of someone trying to deal with the dining room door. Then there was a crash as the kitchen window went.

"Damn. I never thought to lock the kitchen door." Neil said.

Someone was now trying the get through the middle partition door.

The phone rang and Roger picked up the receiver.

"Who are you?" The voice was recognisable.

"Williams, Inspector. We're under siege."

"You're supposed to be dead."

"So Lionel just told me."

"Go to the door and shout 'Operation fourth key is cancelled, call base'.

The central door was in danger of splintering.

Roger walked into the hall and shouted.

"Operation fourth key is cancelled, call base. Inspector Dutton's orders."

They sat in silence as they listened. Sirens of Police cars were arriving and someone from the porch went out to a vehicle in the driveway.

"He's talking on a radio." Janine said, from her view down the side of the net curtain.

The pounding on the internal door had stopped.

With his eyes now accustomed to the dark, Roger fetched his suitcase into the office and laid it down to open it.

"What are you doing?" Janine asked.

"Hiding the proof. I don't intend for anyone to take it away from us after all we've been through to get it."

"Lock it in the hidden document drawer in the desk." Neil suggested.

The minutes ticked by and their assailants congregated in the driveway by their black vehicle. Police had arrived and were asking questions. It must have been fifteen minutes later when Janine noticed someone she recognised.

"Inspector Dutton's here." She said.

"Let's hope he hasn't come to arrest us for being alive." Neil said sarcastically.

"We haven't done anything wrong, have we?" Janine worried.

"No, Janine. This is nothing to do with us, they seem to have believed us to be dead. Dutton will explain I'm sure." Roger assured her.

Neil waited until he rang the bell, then saw him look around at the camera and light. He pressed the speaker button.

"You can come in if you promise you're not going to shoot us." Neil said.

"Just let me in Phelps. There's too much to sort out to joke around."

Neil made a meal of unbolting the door to show how secure it was, and let the inspector in.

Roger drew the curtains and Neil put on the light as they entered the office.

Inspector Dutton looked around at them.

"You look brown. I presume you have been abroad somewhere."

"We were told to go on holiday, so we went."

"To Gibraltar where it was thought you came to a watery grave."

"What made you think that?"

"I expect Lionel will be here in the morning, I'll let him inform you. This was his operation."

The police were obliged to leave somebody on duty in the house until they were able to organise repairs to the broken windows and damaged doors, during which time the house was cold. Trying to sleep was impossible, especially for Janine, which meant Roger was also up all night.

Once again Lionel was there at breakfast time.

"We'll allocate you a permanent place at the table, shall we?" Neil joked. He was the only one who had slept at all.

"I would prefer not to need to visit you on such a regular basis." Lionel retorted.

"Rather here than in your offices." Roger muttered.

"At least you are protected in our offices, Mr Williams." Lionel said with some sarcasm.

"We thought we were safe here." Janine said.

"It appears not. Although this time it was my men, next time it may not be. I would suggest some kind of lockable shutters, especially at the back of the house. You do appear to be vulnerable in places and you seem to incite problems even if unintentionally."

"Tell me about it." Neil said darkly.

Lionel looked at him through lowered eyelids.

They moved to the office on Roger's suggestion. Janine opened the filing cabinet and took out the agreement, placing it on the desk. Lionel picked it up and read it.

"How inventive of you. I understand you found Mr Blenkinsop."

"How did you know?" Neil asked.

"I went to Gibraltar. Your new friend the Lieutenant was worried when you disappeared. But perhaps you were unaware of what happened. Tell me about how you escaped."

Roger began. "It was because of Janine, someone pushed her into the swimming pool."

"Yes, two boys, I know about that. I did wonder if it was a deliberate attack. Of course, at the time I had no knowledge of the boat you were interested in. That came from your Lieutenant."

"He deserves a medal. Without him we wouldn't have the proof. You know about our trip to Tarifa, then?"

"Yes. I understand it was successful. Do you have the proof, I would be interested in seeing it?"

Janine, who was sitting behind the desk, opened the hidden compartment under the desk top and slid forward the photographs. Lionel took them and spent some time perusing them.

"The Guardia seemed to believe that it was the blow to the head which killed him and the mark around his neck was caused by a neck chain being caught and pulled off in the water. Percy Blenkinsop would not have been wearing a neck chain." Roger stared at Lionel who looked between him and the photographs.

"Did they believe it was an accident?"

"No. All the tags had been cut from his clothing to prevent any identification."

"Why would they leave a neck chain?" He looked down at the photograph again. "He was garrotted."

"I would say so. You said Southam told you which boat."

"He did. They were searching for you and it left port with you three missing."

"You thought they had murdered us too?" Roger asked.

"You were obviously too far away to know. The boat sank in a storm on the Wednesday night. We thought you were on it. There was no evidence to prove otherwise."

"You expected us to go on board, knowing what we did about them?"

"Not willingly, but they were holed, possibly by something in a compartment, we thought it could be you. There was a commotion on the boat the night before they left. You haven't explained how you knew which boat or how you knew to escape."

"That was due to Janine." Roger said. Lionel looked over at her.

"Janine does appear to be a very significant part of your agency." Lionel noted. Janine blushed.

"She was really upset after falling in the water. Apparently, she lashed out at the doctor who saved her and she felt bad about it and didn't go to dinner. She was in her room with the window open and heard them. Our rooms were downstairs, just above the water, and they came down the walkway below, talking. Probably Eli and Sergio. Sergio was suggesting pushing one of us off a balcony to look like and accident. When we got back from the trip to Tarifa at three in the morning she was waiting. We packed our cases and ran. We knew they were looking for us and weren't about to hang around. We were in Spain by first light on the Tuesday morning."

"Did you know which boat before you left England? We lost track of you until you turned up in Gibraltar."

"We knew the Abrams had a boat and something the secretary at the Abrams estate agent said to Janine led us to Gosport. We knew which boat because of Neil. He can tell you."

Lionel looked at Neil who had been letting Roger take over as usual.

"It was only because Roger had this hunch about finding Mrs Blenkinsop. Everyone where we came from left a key hidden in the front garden and it turned out she was no different. There wasn't a scrap of paperwork in the house, no letters, nothing. It was as if someone had already been there and cleared it out. A neighbour had been in and picked up the post. It was because of the letter from Worksop, it was dated from when Mrs Blenkinsop should have been there with her sister. I didn't open it, but I picked it up and there was a postcard from Percy, posted in Lisbon. It even gave the name of the boat."

Lionel was silent as he took in what Neil had said.

Janine leaned forward on the desk. "Is there any news about Mrs Blenkinsop."

Lionel turned his attention to her.

"Indeed. She went to visit her sister, but after a disagreement she left. That was the reason for the letter. Luckily for her she never went home. She visited her late husband's sister instead."

"She's safe! That is good to hear." Roger beamed at Janine. "You need to realise, Lionel, we only kept going because Janine asked how we would feel if you found her alive and we had to tell her we hadn't bothered searching."

"Janine again. Never believe you are only the office staff, Miss Mathers. Every one of you has a role to play. I believe I have said before that it is because all three of you work as a team that you are successful. We did indeed find Mrs Blenkinsop alive. Once we knew for certain that Percy was dead, we informed her that he died when the boat foundered off the straits of Gibraltar." He picked up the photograph from the cemetery. "You even know where he is buried. Perhaps she would like to visit, it will help to bring closure for her."

All three of them looked at him in surprise.

"We are not so heartless that we don't understand. The poor woman has lost her son, and knowing he was murdered will bring her no peace. To allow her to believe he died in a boating accident doing what he loved is the most humane option. We are never going to be able to prosecute those involved, they are all dead."

"What about Sir Amos?" Roger asked.

"Sir Amos has been removed, that is all you need to know." He stood up to leave and picked up the photographs. "You will be paid, I will make sure of that. I will be in touch in a day or so. Someone needs to escort Mrs Blenkinsop to visit her son's grave."

Neil leaned forward. "If we were supposed to be dead, why the stakeout?"

Lionel sat down again.

"I'm afraid we made use of your empty house. Those involved do not know we thought you dead, they expected you to return. We are of the opinion there is someone we have not yet found. Possibly from the army. We let them believe you had knowledge and it appears you did, as you turned up in Gibraltar knowing the name of the boat. We will need to keep the house under surveillance. I am sorry about that, I imagine you expected to return to a quiet haven."

"So we are sitting ducks!" Roger exclaimed.

"That was why I suggested you might accompany Mrs Blenkinsop to see the grave of her son. It would be closure for her and hopefully for you. I don't expect them to wait too long. We will give them a little prod, let them know you are home."

"I don't want to go back to Spain." Neil said. "I'll find somewhere else to go."

"Such as?" Lionel stared coldly at him.

"I could climb Snowdon or go walking in the Welsh hills. I'm getting soft, all this sitting about."

"Neil…" Roger began.

"Forget it. I need some time on my own and exercise is good for me. I've missed the army routine. Go back to Spain and enjoy the warmth. I'll be in a better mood when you get back."

Neil picked up his rucksack and carried it upstairs to unpack.

"You have a problem." Lionel informed them.

"Neil is feeling hurt, that's all. To do with a girl on holiday. Her father phoned an army friend in England to check up on him and was told he was discharged for killing someone."

"It is going to take time for them to accept what happened. I can understand Phelps' anger, the Army should have amended their records."

"He thinks he can't get a job anywhere because they would ask for a reference from the Army."

"Does he want a job. Is he not happy here?"

"That's hard to say at the moment. I think he'll calm down in a day or two. Perhaps climbing a mountain would be good for him." Roger surmised.

Janine was looking distressed. "I didn't realise he was that upset. I know he liked her and I've never known him have a girlfriend before."

Lionel left them feeling bereft. All the excitement of the chase was over and they were left with the problem of repairing their home while still being under threat.

Their case load was nil and the future seemed empty.

"Don't worry," Roger said. "Something will turn up soon enough. Perhaps we need a holiday to recuperate from the holiday." He said.

EPILOGUE

ady Herbert was brought in to answer a few questions about her husband's associates. She was adamant that she knew of none. She asked what her husband had been accused of and was told they had evidence linking him with a crime involving his sister and brother in law, evidence which had been found by a private detective agency. Just for the moment, everyone was being left to believe the Abrams were on their way to South America, including their son Ephraim who was being kept under surveillance. There was a tap on his phone but they were not hopeful of it being of use.

The order to deliver the armaments to Mountbeck House had been signed by an officer who was denying it was his signature. The driver had been posted abroad and was now recuperating in hospital. Once he was well enough to talk, he gave them the name of the corporal who had been with him and handled the paperwork. He thought it a strange place for a weapons dump but he had delivered there previously. The paperwork had looked in order and there was a Major and a Corporal there to help them unload.

As Lionel had hoped, Lady Herbert telephoned her nephew and told him what had been said, after which he was tailed to a public phone box.

* * *

Bookings were made for three nights at a hotel in Malaga and a hire car was arranged. As it was urgent for them to be away from the house, Janine and Roger were encouraged to stay in Barnsley while they helped Mrs Blenkinsop obtain a passport.

Less than a week after they had returned, Roger and Janine were on their way back to Spain. Roger drove to Tarifa and found the beach where Percy had been found. Being October now, the weather had been unsettled and the sea was whipped up into white horses, enough for her to believe the story about the foundering of the boat.

Roger found a restaurant where they could feed her something other than churros, after which he took them to the cemetery.

He wondered if there had been any information sent to the Guardia Civil as there was an officer standing to one side as they entered. The white edifice which contained the body of Percy was now fronted by a marble plaque bearing his name, date of birth and death, and an oval picture frame with his photograph. Mrs Blenkinsop leaned against Janine and cried. Roger noted that Janine was also crying. Everything they had done had been like an exercise, it had not felt real. Even when they had visited before, both Roger and Neil had been tired and relieved to find an answer. Now it was very real. Here was a mother who had lost her son and they had found him for her. Roger felt humbled. It had been Janine who had insisted they find him for his mother, and she had been right.

For the rest of their time in Spain they treated her as the mother neither of them had.

* * *

Neil had left first, taking suitable clothing and shoes for walking and climbing. He also took a copy of the addresses from Roger's book and the flick-knife, carefully wrapped.

There would be plenty of time when he had sorted his problem.

They weren't hard to find, he never even had to ask. Even the neighbours on the council estate avoided them, and their parents made no attempt to control them. They were a law unto themselves and roamed the area spreading fear wherever they went. None of them worked. Neil wondered where they got all the money they spent on drink.

The first night he spent watching from dark alleys, learning their favourite pubs, following them as they terrorised the area. The big one, he was the biggest bully, anyone arguing with him was punched into silence. The knife man was the most dangerous, he sliced at anyone who dared to defend themselves.

How was he going to do this? He only had one knife.

They were drunk, excessively so. The third member of their cabal was being sick in an alley. Knifeman was swearing at him while he followed the bully who was lumbering away, ignoring him. Neil stepped into the alley and stood behind him, brought the knife round his neck and stabbed.

When he never appeared, bully went to find his friend and found him slumped on the floor, blood pouring from his neck. He was drowning in it, the knife still sticking embedded in his neck. He turned on knifeman.

"You bastard. What has he ever done to you?" He pulled the knife from his neck and stabbed at knifeman, who retaliated with his own knife.

It may have been possible to save at least one of them if they had been found in time. Those who passed by the alley saw them lying there and thought them drunk, no-one was willing to go anywhere near them. When they were found the following morning, there was no hope of saving even knifeman. His prints were on both knives plus the bully's on the knife that killed knifeman.

The area never mourned them, it just became a much pleasanter place to live.

Neil only wished he knew who Fiona's father had phoned. But he had no intention of making a habit of this. This was for Roger and Janine. When he had needed them, they had been there for him. Now they needed him if they were to have a future free from fear. He hoped he had just given them one.

WHAT ACTUALLY HAPPENED

Mandarina III left Gibraltar later than she had intended. They had searched for the three missing young people for long enough. The Caleta receptionist had thought they must have booked out as their passports were gone. The night receptionist had remembered phoning for a taxi to the airport, but they were not listed as being on a flight out. The only passengers were already pre-booked by the tour company. They must have gone through the border to Spain but they found no taxi who had picked up three young people on the Spanish side of the border.

Johnjo didn't understand why they were so intent on finding them and was beginning to be worried by the intensity of their search. They had obviously only been looking for a friend and must have misunderstood which boat he was on. The Adams were regular visitors, and although Sergio worried him a little, he wouldn't like to cause them any trouble. So he said nothing when a naval officer came asking about them.

They stayed for two days and would have stayed another day or two rather than leaving so late in the day, but the weather forecast showed possible storms and high winds in the next few days, which would leave the straits uncomfortably rough.

Eli had phoned his son and had no response, so he phoned his brother-in-law, Sir Amos. He spoke to his wife, who was bemused as to why her husband had been taken in for questioning by someone important. She had no idea where he was and he had been gone several days. They weren't dressed as police, she said.

There were recriminations when he went back to the boat. Someone must have said something. Sergio was very angry, he had made sure there was no-one with any information who could track them, so he blamed someone in Eli's family.

If they had been discovered it would mean prison. At least they had abolished the death penalty, although that could have been better than a lifetime in a cell. Their only option was to run. They had made tentative arrangements for an escape route, although the South Atlantic would be difficult this late in the year.

During the Wednesday morning, they had acquired all the containers they could and filled them with fuel, hopefully sufficient to get them to safety. When the weather forecast came in they were left with no option, staying for days in Gibraltar would leave them open to arrest.

Once they were out of sight of Gibraltar the water was already choppy, but nothing worse than they had weathered before. It was only to be expected in the straits.

Just at the moment they could still see the receding coastline on either side. They needed to be in clear water before it became too dark.

They were aware of a patrol boat circling in the area.

"Are they following us?"

"I don't think so. They're just on patrol. They look like the one we normally see."

The patrol boat circled them, coming quite close as they passed.

Sergio was having trouble with the steering.

"Something's the matter. She's not answering to the helm. Will you take over, Eli? I'll go and see what the problem is."

Sergio returned within seconds.

"We're holed. We're taking in water. We'll need to get to a port urgently. Can we signal the patrol boat?"

They tried flashing the big flashlight. They called on the radio but they were still tuned into the Gibraltar.

"We're holed and going down. There's a patrol boat near but we can't make them understand." He shouted down the radio.

"Put up a flare, Sergio."

The sky was darkening fast as the flare went up, lighting the whole area. The patrol boat was quite close and in the brightness of the light Sergio saw something streaking towards them through the water.

The wreckage was washed up on both shores. There was nobody to see the explosion that caused it, not even the patrol boat speeding away from them, back to where it had originated. Nobody ever mentioned anyone having been anywhere near when it happened.